# DEAD END

Stenski, a lonely, gaunt Czech, had worked for the British in Berlin for twenty years, creating an intelligence network. And a Russian broke it up, piece by piece, until only a little Englishman remained, a timid Englishman who went walking a dog one night and was beaten to death. From that moment, Stenski began the last operation — to lure the Russian to the West, interrogate and discredit him. At least, that was what everyone thought.

CHRISTOPHER HILTON

# DEAD END

*Complete and Unabridged*

# LINFORD
*Leicester*

First published in Great Britain in 1978 by
Robert Hale Limited
London

First Linford Edition
published 2004
by arrangement with
Robert Hale Limited
London

British Library CIP Data

Hilton, Christopher
   Dead end.—Large print ed.—
   Linford mystery library
   1. Detective and mystery stories
   2. Large type books
   I. Title
   823.9'14 [F]

   ISBN 1–84395–125–8

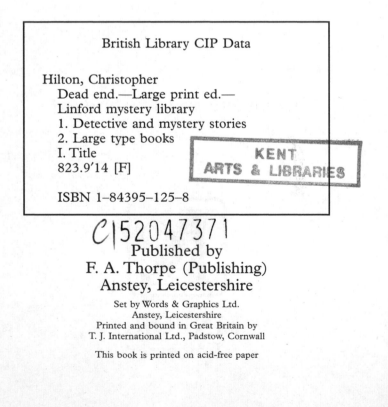

Published by
F. A. Thorpe (Publishing)
Anstey, Leicestershire

Set by Words & Graphics Ltd.
Anstey, Leicestershire
Printed and bound in Great Britain by
T. J. International Ltd., Padstow, Cornwall

This book is printed on acid-free paper

# Preface

British people are taught from a very early age that, as a race, there are certain things they will not do. Further, they are guided by a touchingly simple belief that what they have actually done, however callous it may appear, has been done under the sting of necessity; and with justice on their side. If you want to prove the fallacy of it, nothing could be easier: Open any history book.

The theme of this story was suggested — and no more than that — by a paratrooper, still in his teens when he was parachuted into the Dutch town of Arnhem. That was the very first time he had seen how British people can behave, and, of his overall memory of that great and dreadful operation, certain moments haunt him still, thirty years on.

The story is not about Arnhem, nor anything like it; but some of the sentiments have been drawn from that

1

particularly well.

The title came to me when I happened to be in an aeroplane crossing the Pacific. Dead End seemed very apt during those hours, for me as well as the story. I've always been a nervous sort of person when travelling at 500 miles an hour 30,000 feet up — and helpless.

# Part One

# The October City

He came from the U-bahn station on foot, a hollow figure in an old coat. The yellow taxi cabs were waiting in a line at the kerbside but the drivers ignored him and kept on reading their newspapers. He didn't look a customer.

Rain had fallen some time before, dragged across from the Low Countries on the winds of autumn; and it had left the first dampness of winter in the air. A handful of women meandered down Mariendorferdamm, some carrying shopping bags: It was the awkward, empty hour between lunch and the schoolchildren coming home. A single tram passed, its antenna clinging to the web of overhead wires, stopped in front of the U-bahn to let a few people off, a few people on; and went away, back into the faltering traffic which was funnelled through road works towards Olendorf.

He walked like a man who did not

know the area and was feeling his way from landmark to landmark to his destination: the new church at the corner of Britzerstrasse, darkened in the grey, failing light; the technical college half way down Rixdorferstrasse, with ranks of students at desks glimpsed through the windows.

He walked slowly and drawn in upon himself, as if he feared the rain would come back.

The road sign was blue: Krankenhaus 500 metres. He saw the complex of modern buildings from a distance, every window ablaze with light like a ship on fire. It was set back into a couple of acres of lawns with elm trees planted here and there. The long car park, running down one side of the building, was only half full. Inside the main gate there were more signs, small, white wooden arrows pointing to the various departments along the tarmac paths between the trees. He went straight to the main entrance. It must have served for casualties, too, because, under a flat, protruding roof, stretchers and wheelchairs were stacked ready.

The glass doors opened automatically at his footfall and he walked across the reception area to a cubicle marked: Information. Far down a corridor which stretched away to the wards, nurses in clinical white moved noiselessly across the polished floor. A middle-aged woman sat at a desk in the cubicle with two heaps of dossiers in front of her and a white telephone at her elbow.

He looked up at the wall-clock, encased in glass. Thirteen minutes to three. He was early, but that didn't matter. The woman gazed without curiosity at his thin face, the skin tightened back onto the cheekbones. He looked most un-German, but that was hardly surprising. The country was full of foreign workers, and he could certainly have passed for an elderly Balkan labourer. She said nothing.

'I want the mortuary. It is not indicated on the signs.'

'You must go back out of the main entrance and turn left. It is situated behind this building, in the trees.'

He felt the wind press against his face as he came out — these hospitals are

7

always so hot, he thought, like incubators — and he followed the path round to the back. There was a single sign there, and very small, like an apology in a newspaper: Necessary but irritating. The mortuary was redbrick and without windows, camouflaged by an arc of the elm trees a discreet distance from the hospital itself. The path led to a metal door and he had to ring the bell twice before a young man in a white overall came.

'I'm from the embassy. The British Embassy. I rang you this morning.'

'You must be Mr. Simpson.'

Stenski nodded.

'Follow me.'

The door closed behind him, and they went down a narrow passage. Stenski noticed a thick and unpleasant smell, like an unction, in the air. The walls were hardboard partitions which did not reach the ceiling and the lighting, arc lamps suspended from cross beams, served for all the rooms. They stopped at a door marked number five, and the young man opened it with a key. He stood back, gesturing for Stenski to go in first.

It was a very small, square room, no bigger than a bedroom in a cheap hotel. The walls were painted cream and, against the pure white of the young man's overall, they looked curiously soiled.

The body was on a low, metal trolley with a sheet draped over it. Stenski was not deluded. They stored them in frozen vaults, and wheeled them out into these rooms specially when anyone wanted to see one.

'I suppose you want to have a look?' The young man wore thick spectacles and blond hair lay down his forehead almost to their rim.

Stenski nodded again.

The man drew back the sheet until it lay, crumpled, across the feet of the body; stepped away and, for an instant, contemplated it — that was his trade, after all — and indicated with a sweep of his hand that Stenski could now come forward. As Stenski did so, he went to a corner of the room and stood, motionless, just watching. Stenski sensed immediately that he wasn't watching the body now:

He was watching him.

Stenski thought only: He knows I'm a Jew, and he wants to see me revolted. He'll probably enjoy that. He didn't even warn me what condition the body was in.

It was true that the body was grotesque. The cranium had been partly crushed, the neck broken and twisted but still holding the head by the chords of the throat. The rib cage has been beaten in on the left side. At least they had sponged the blood away, and the eyes had been tactfully closed.

'We have not had time to apply any cosmetics yet,' the man said. Evidently he found Stenski's visit boring or in some way inconvenient. 'He will not look like that when his relatives see him.' He paused. 'Have you seen enough?' And he came forward and lifted the sheet back with a practiced movement. 'The police have all his particulars. They took all his papers away, also his wallet. His clothes are in the office, in a parcel.'

Stenski made no observation.

'They found him in the Volkspark, although I expect you know that already.

10

He was walking a neighbour's dog, and when the dog came back by itself they went out to look for him. He was in some bushes, or may be near them. I don't really know.' They moved out of the room back into the passage, and the man locked the door again. 'There is the question of the disposal of the body. That concerns you, since his identification card suggests he was English.'

'British.'

The young man shrugged. He didn't care, either way.

'We shall have to consult his relatives,' Stenski said. 'He was resident here, but all his family live in the United Kingdom. They may wish the body to be flown back.'

They had begun to walk towards the door.

'You are permitted fourteen days to arrange this, under the regulations. Please be so good as to inform the mortuary controller, Herr Geisler. You have the telephone number, of course.'

They reached the door.

'Do you know something,' the young

11

man said — it was not a question, and it was never intended to be one — 'When they brought the body in last night, and I examined it, there was a conclusion which I could not help reaching. This man, Atkins the police say his name was, had been crudely beaten to death. I am a qualified mortician, but anybody could have seen that. He had been beaten by something heavy. It's not so unusual, not unusual at all, as these things go.' His hand reached towards the door. 'But the beating continued long after he was dead. It must have done. Why would anybody want to do that?'

When Stenski came out, it was raining again, gently.

\*　\*　\*

'I'm going to London. There is a plane at seven,' Stenski said quietly.

The room, on the second floor of the Embassy annex, was too small. They had been moved in years before on a temporary basis and had stayed. The single, curtained window gave onto an enclosed courtyard with a leafless tree in the middle of it.

The walls of the room were perfectly bare except of a map of Berlin placed above the gas fire; and, by the secretary's typewriter, some postcards cellotaped to the frosted pane of glass which separated the room from the corridor outside. Stenski had hung his coat on a peg behind the door. He wore a black suit which had looked just short of shabby for an age; narrow legs and turn-ups.

He always wore white shirts with the collars just too large — for a manufacturer he was, no doubt, a difficult size, and he would never have had shirts made for him; but the collars did give his neck the appearance of being too thin, as if it might not have the strength to support the head. He wore plain ties which he rotated according to some unknown criterion. It was all just the right blending. People did not notice him.

Johnson had come in and sat at this desk. 'I'm sorry,' he said to Stenski after a long, difficult pause. 'I'm very sorry.'

He was generations younger than

Stenski; 30, maybe 35, with fair, curly hair and a fresh face which seemed to acquire another dimension of youth whenever he was near Stenski.

Stenski stood up. His desk was strewn with newspapers from both halves of the city, east and west. He walked urgently to the window. 'It's all over,' he whispered, as if he was talking only to himself. The statement lacked any kind of emotion: It was no more and no less than the recognition of a fact, as a doctor may diagnose an illness — even a terminal illness — without any feeling of personal involvement. But it was a curiously detached evaluation for any man discussing himself. 'Have you seen the papers?' Stenski wondered absently.

'I have.'

'What an advertisement!' He held his hands behind his back like a schoolmaster. 'People in our line of business work for different reasons . . . but they work on trust. Trust that we will protect them in some way. They hardly expect to see reports in newspapers.' He returned to his desk. An opened notebook lay across the papers with a lead pencil on it. He had written nothing. 'There is not very much of the network left,' he said. 'Just a few stragglers, pimps, most of them, I shouldn't wonder.'

He spoke English with a heavy accent which sometimes masked the correctness of the construction as if, in a way which one could never define, he was fluent in it but not altogether comfortable. And there remained, like sores which would never go away, certain basic sounds which he could not formulate. He had long ceased the struggle.

He was restless. He went back to the window and looked down into the courtyard. The wind was gathering the fallen leaves, lifting them in whirlpools, releasing them and scattering them in a shifting mosaic across the cobblestones.

'People aren't going to want to work for us any more,' he said. 'Who can blame them?' He answered his own question. 'Nobody can blame them.'

Johnson was thinking back over two years. It had all begun so stupidly — with a rumour; a rumour about changes in the

MVD infrastructure. Nobody in Berlin or London paid much attention. Some people feed off rumours. Stenski always preferred to wait. Then Markov was appointed. Even London hadn't really heard of him. That had been apparent immediately. He had emerged from the anonymous reaches of the Russian civil service; as a matter of record, he had been a director of the Ministry for the Distribution of Foodstuffs.

That background looked unlikely to produce a man to run the MVD East European operations and the feeling in the west was that he had got it purely on his administrative abilities.

For three months, nothing happened. Stenski was suspicious. But he was content to wait. Then a contact vanished in East Berlin, vanished as if he had never been there. He went to bed one evening in his flat and was not present at dawn.

'That,' Stenski had announced, 'is the beginning. I know it. I smell it. I taste it.' He had been standing by the same embassy window. The tree had been covered in foliage.

Then it was Jungermann, killed in a car accident along the corridor between West Berlin and West Germany. The word was that he had swerved to avoid a lorry, gone down the embankment and ploughed into the trees, thirty kilometres away from Magdeburg; then Manstein, who defected. He went east one day and did not return.

'Markov?' Stenski would say. 'We're all technicians, all of us; but he's got intuition. That's the difference.'

Now Atkins.

'Why don't we go over to Artur's Keller and I'll buy you a stiff drink?' Johnson asked optimistically. 'And you could get something to eat.'

'You go,' Stenski said. 'I'll stay here.' He was still locked in his posture at the window, watching the leaves. 'Margeurite can get me some sandwiches when she comes back.'

★  ★  ★

When Johnson returned, Margeurite was typing intently. Stenski had not eaten.

Normally he left great quantities of crumbs across his desk which, when he had gone, Margeurite would brush up under protest; but there were none. The newspapers had been thrust into a wastepaper basket and Stenski's desk was clear except for the notebook and the pencil. Still he had written nothing.

'You haven't had any sandwiches,' Johnson began. Stenski gazed at him and made a limp, hopeless gesture with his right hand, though whether food had been prevented by lack of appetite or simply circumstances was not apparent.

'You know where I spent some time while you were over the road, Paul?' The use of the Christian name signified that he was about to say something important. He did not employ the English habit of surnames, and normally did not address Johnson by name at all. 'I've been down in the records. Looking for something I remembered from years ago. Before you came here. A file, actually. It isn't here any more. Everything back past 1960 went in the last purge. You know what those people are like, don't you? You understand their mentality. They probably just threw everything out. As if you can pick an arbitrary date and throw everything away on one side of it, keep everything on the other. Damn people. What was so sacred about 1960 anyway?'

He lifted the pencil, then laid it down again as if it had suddenly become heavy. 'They are just filing clerks, those people. They dress them up with titles and little offices, but that doesn't alter one damn thing: They're filing clerks.'

The wind was getting up, moaning very softly against the windowpane.

'They did say that some of the more interesting — that was their word, typical of bureaucrats — files had been transferred to London, but they had not bothered to keep a note of which. I've been thinking of asking London to institute a search over there for the file.'

'What file did you want?'

'Just a file.' He could be mysterious when he wished. 'Just something to support an idea. I'm not going to let go, you see. Not yet. I'm going to do something to Markov which will be a great deal more unpleasant than anything he has done to me.'

He coughed.

'That's why I'm on the seven o'clock plane.' He was watching Johnson, gauging his reaction. The old eyes were sharp as a predatory bird. 'I have decided to go to London myself and discuss it. And look for the file.'

'Maybe you won't come back,' Johnson said. 'You might be replaced on the spot.'

'Perhaps.'

The thin fingers closed the notebook. The pencil rolled away and came to rest half way across the desk. There was a long silence.

That was Tuesday — and the last day of October.

# Part Two

# The November Exit

He came back on Thursday looking, as he always did when he had been away, furtive and servile. He must have taken the morning flight from London but had not rung from Tempelhof, simply caught the airport bus to the terminal and walked to the Embassy.

He said something very softly as he came into the room — it might almost have been a sigh — which neither Johnson nor Margeurite heard properly, took his coat laboriously off, a slow ritual which demanded a series of movements of hunching and arching the shoulder-blades, and sat at his desk.

He made a telephone call to the big German woman whose husband was caretaker at his block of apartments, to be sure that everything was in order.

'But,' she said, 'You did not say that you would be away for so long. I made some supper for you yesterday evening.

You did not come.'

'Never mind,' Stenski said. He made no attempt to placate the woman, who he disliked. He sounded tired.

'Did you bring me a little gift back?' she asked.

'Yes.'

Her voice fluttered in bogus excitement. He put the telephone down quickly, and Margeurite took him his mail, a few letters which he scanned without opening. He gathered them, as a dealer will gather playing cards, in a symmetrical pile and laid them carefully at a corner of his desk.

'We're moving on,' he said at length to Johnson. 'You and I. If you agree of course, but I'm afraid I rather took that for granted.'

'Moving where?'

Stenski ignored that. 'They are sending somebody here to find out who killed Atkins. After that, they will make a permanent appointment. It will be only one man, not two. I suppose that is an implied criticism of us, among many others.'

Margeurite was typing regardless. 'The man is called Barnard. I did not meet him, but I gather he has established some sort of reputation for finding things out. London are very confident he will find out who killed Atkins. He comes tomorrow.'

Johnson felt a kind of pity then, for a man grown quickly old and worthless.

'Margeurite, you must make up your own mind about your future, but I think they would prefer you to leave, or at least go to another department within the Embassy. They are going to leave the permanent appointment to be the judge of that.'

She stopped typing and lit a tipped cigarette. 'That's nice of them,' she said, her voice heavy with English sarcasm. 'Very nice.'

She put on the kettle, and Stenski began to open his letters with a paper knife, methodically.

★   ★   ★

Barnard did ring from Tempelhof and said he wanted an Embassy car to collect him. Johnson took the call, and told him it would be quicker to take a taxi. Barnard was unhappy about that. He must have been expecting some kind of reception.

'You knew I was coming. Didn't London advise you of the flight number and E.T.A.?'

'A most distasteful man,' Stenski observed. 'I am going out now. I have no desire to meet him, although I am afraid he is bound to want to meet me. That would be indispensible, looking at it from his point of view. I am sure you can cope with him.' Johnson began to protest. 'Treat him with diffidence,' Stenski said. 'He might be hostile. In fact, I am sure he will be.'

Half an hour later, Barnard arrived. He knocked once and entered the room without waiting to be invited. That set the tone.

'Sorry about the car,' Johnson said. 'Like a cup of tea?'

Barnard looked round, noticing the kettle on the formica table, the three mugs nearby, the opened packet of sugar, the fire, the postcards.

'Cosy little nook,' he observed. 'A little bit of civilisation among the barbarians.'

He was medium height, and powerfully built. His shoulders were square, his neck thick. His face was florid, and very small tufts of hair protruded from his ears. He looked as if he liked a drink. Brown hair covered the backs of his hands; his fingers were red, a deeper shade than his face. He wore a tartan sports jacket and flannels; and heavy brown shoes with laces, done up in tight knots. He might have been a prison warder; the kind who wouldn't stand any backchat.

Johnson opened the bottom drawer of his desk and produced a hip-size bottle of scotch. 'Something stronger than tea? We get it duty free.' It seemed the right gesture.

'Not till the sun goes down. Not that you get much sun up here, if my memory serves me.' He had an overcoat slung over his arm. 'Which bloody architect designed this place anyway?' He motioned with his free arm, meaning the Embassy complex. 'He must have been squint-eyed at least. It looks more like a mausoleum than an Embassy. I suppose that's not inappropriate.' He grunted. That might have been his laugh. Or not.

'Got accommodation?' Johnson asked.

'Sure,' Barnard said. 'All fixed up by London. Small hotel not too far way. At least, it had better not be too far away.'

'Been to Berlin before?'

He nodded. 'Long time ago. When things were nasty.' He sat on the edge of Stenski's desk, dangling his feet carelessly, like a bather on a rock with his feet in the water.

'Most of the time I was da druben — over there, in West Germany.'

'Army?'

'Something like that. Any more questions?'

'None that you'd want to answer.'

'Don't get clever with me. I don't like it.'

Barnard lit a cigarette and brought Margeurite's ashtray over to Stenski's desk, placing it by his hip as he sat again. He waved the cigarette at Johnson. 'Duty free.' Johnson shrugged. 'I left my suitcase down with the commissionaire. I suppose it's safe down there?' He did laugh this time, and Johnson noticed that he had a perfect set of teeth; probably false. Barnard grew expansive. 'Tell you what I'm going to do — and what I'm going to do is very important to you, because London have told me to expect full co-operation, anytime I want it, day or night — I'm going to find the hotel, have a shower, have a long beer. Then I'm going to come back here, and you and I are going to have a very detailed talk about poor old Atkins and his accident.

'Where's Stenski? Run away, I suppose. We're also, in case you're wondering, going to talk about him. Interesting history. Prisoner of war, you know. Very bright before the war, college in some place called Levoca, studying dentistry. Spoke Czech, Slovak, some German and Russian — the Russian border wasn't that far away. The Ukraine, actually. I have a reputation for being thorough,' Barnard said. 'A dying art.' The tone of his voice altered, moving back to the recital of knowledge. 'There is some suggestion of collaboration when the Germans took him. That's only an inference, naturally, because he survived. Maybe they were impressed — he was only a year away from his degree. They could have used him as the camp dentist.'

Barnard moved his whole arm to flick ash from the cigarette, a precise, practiced movement. 'London told me to move fast,' he said. 'No point in hiding that. We're naked here now — now that they've all gone: Jungermann, Manstein, Atkins . . . ' He drew on the cigarette. 'I'll be back in an hour.'

Barnard was thorough. At first, Johnson imagined him to be purely slow-witted; but that was quite false. Barnard wanted to know everything, and he wrote a great deal in a blue-backed notebook which he kept in his jacket pocket. They talked across Johnson's desk. Outside, night had fallen and the office workers had gone: Barnard was still moving stubbornly through fact after fact. He looked the kind who would have gone on until dawn if he'd wanted.

One name interested him immediately: Gause. Johnson had talked briefly about him, and his name was on several files, even in London: The commercial traveller from the east.

'I want to meet him,' Barnard said, adding imperiously: 'Fix it.' Johnson shrugged.

'Fix it quickly. Tell him to come over if you have to. But get him here.'

Johnson nodded.

★　★　★

They met two days later, at half past five outside the bus station at Schoneberg. Barnard had hired a car. Gause was standing under a street lamp, a briefcase in his left hand, close to the public toilets. As Barnard drew up, he stepped forward from the shadows, briskly opened the passenger door when he saw the headlights dipped twice in quick succession, and sat. A few heads turned from a nearby queue, but that was only curiosity.

Barnard drove back to the main road, heading out on the long, straight track towards Charlottenburg and the open country.

'We're going somewhere quiet,' Barnard said.

'All right.' The briefcase was on his lap, and he had draped his hands protectively over it. He wore a dark-brown, dome-shaped fur hat which came almost down to his ears. 'But I don't have much time. An hour, maybe an hour and a half. Nothing more.' He spoke with the American accent and the American construction. 'If I'm late going back over tonight, they get very edgy on the border and start wondering just what I've been doing.'

Barnard nodded. The traffic was heavy and he had hardly had a chance to look away to the figure next to him; had only observed, in the last lingerings of the twilight, a tall man with eyes sunk far back into the head and masked by the thick lenses of his spectacles.

At Pichelsdorf, the traffic released them and they could see the wall to their left among the pine trees. A thousand metres ahead, it crudely bisected the road itself but Barnard turned off before they reached it, before even they had drawn

32

level with the high, white board which said in English, French and Russian that they were leaving the American sector.

They were in a lane now, threaded through the trees with pic-nic areas and oil drums for litter. He stopped in a clearing on high ground, just off the lane. Far below, through the trees, the wall could be seen very clearly: High wire mesh here, not breeze blocks at all, with a strip of land cleared away on both sides of it and, on the eastern side, bales of barbed wire with, behind them, the pylons which held the arc lamps. And, behind that again, the concrete strip which was the patrol road.

In the distance, a log watch-tower rose above the trees, a tapering structure lashed together at the joints by rope. A ladder travelled up the centre of it to the cabin on the platform. But it was too far away for anyone in it to have seen the Rekord with much precision, even if they had been looking through binoculars.

Barnard switched off the ignition and

all the lights. 'Glad you got my message,' he said.

Gause ignored it. 'What happened to Atkins?'

'I'd like to know that, too.'

'Christ,' he said. 'It was a safe little operation. I collected the stuff in East Berlin and just brought it over. The Vopos at the checkpoint know me. All right, they change the shifts at the checkpoint, deliberately mix them up a bit, but I knew all the Vopos, listen, I used to do their shopping for them, nylons, blue jeans, scotch, pop records. They didn't even bother to check me a lot of the time, just waved me through.

'I always come over on a Tuesday, and at the same time. They like that. They like the regularity.' He was beginning to get excited. 'Atkins? He was all right, that one. He never made a fuss. He always called me Arthur.'

Gause looked hard at Barnard. 'It was just like we were old buddies.'

'How much money did he give you?'

'At the start, 200 marks each time.'

'Federal marks, not East German marks?'

'Of course. What the hell do you think? DDR marks are not available here, anyway.'

'And you've a bank account here in West Berlin . . . '

'You be damn careful what you say.' His eyes seemed to swell behind the spectacles.

'I have the account number, a full statement of every payment, every withdrawal, every comma and every fullstop. I'm not here on vacation.'

Gause produced a slender pipe and held it without either filling or lighting it.

'Why did you do it?' Barnard asked.

'Where are you from, the Ivy League or something? I told you: the money.'

'But . . . '

'Listen, you listen, that's all.' He leaned over and grasped Barnard by the arm. 'It was a nice little operation, see, a milk run. I was only a courier, I never even knew what was in the packets I brought over, and I didn't care. They didn't need to kill him, that's what I don't understand. If they knew about Atkins, they must have known about me, and if they wanted to stop the operation, and they're working from East Berlin and I live in East Berlin, why didn't they just arrest me and try me in one of those special courts they have?'

He was searching his pockets for tobacco, but not concentrating on the search and not finding any.

Barnard looked away, down to the wire. A khaki coloured jeep was coming along the patrol road on the eastern side with two soldiers in it, slow as a funeral procession. It had no lights on.

Gause said: 'You're new here, you don't know how their minds work. They are cautious, all of them, because they are taught to be cautious. People don't take risks, they keep smiling and say the right things. Those people would never have killed Atkins, especially when they could have crippled the operation by getting me.' He was sweating. 'It's hot in here, too damn hot.' He wound his window down laboriously, and the smoke from Barnard's cigarette was sucked across and out into the chill night air.

'So who did?'

'God knows. And that's the truth. I'm next. I must be. The joke is, I've spent years struggling for that bank account, and just when I've nearly got enough, this.' He shook his head.

'So don't go back over tonight. You don't have to.'

Very slowly, Gause took out an old leather wallet. From it, he drew a photograph of a plump woman with two small girls standing in front of her. It had been taken in a park. 'When I come for good, they come,' he said. 'That's why I haven't been able to rush anything. When I heard about Atkins, I didn't sleep for nights. I would lie there listening to the early morning trams going by, and think: I've almost got enough money, I've almost cheated them, and now they've cheated me.' He motioned with his hand again, towards the lights of a village on the other side. 'You think that is any kind of a life? Compulsory happiness, and no comments invited. Christ, and I damn near cheated them.'

Barnard lit another cigarette. 'So who

did kill him? Come on Gause, you were close to him, you were living with the whole situation. I can make things nasty for you, and that little wife and those girls. I bet they've got wonderful boarding schools over there for kids with no parents, state run and nothing left to chance.'

'Go to hell.'

'Now you listen. I'm going to find out who killed him. I don't much care what happens to you. You're blown anyway, blown sky high. So I'll ask the questions, and you'll answer them, every one to my satisfaction. By the way, you forgot to tell me what your daughters' names are.'

Gause said something obscene. After a long pause he added; 'I'm out now. I wouldn't even have agreed to see you at all except that . . . '

' . . . except that I could do you a great deal of damage. Just by lifting my telephone and ringing the Ministry of Security in East Berlin.'

The jeep was coming back just as slowly, and too far away for them to hear its engine, even with the car window down.

'Let's go back through it,' Barnard said. 'From the beginning.'

'I was born in . . . '

'Not all that. 1960 onwards.'

'All right.' Gause looked at his watch. It was Swiss.

'Nice,' Barnard said. 'A little perk from one of your trips?'

'In 1960, I was a laboratory assistant in a chemical factory in Pankow. Chemicals are very big in East Germany. They call it a primary industry. They liked me. I was never late for work. Within three years I was on the export side. I did the rounds selling chemicals, mostly antibiotics. Poland, Hungary, once to Rumania.'

'Russia?'

Gause shook his head. 'They don't buy things, they only sell things to us.' He smiled bitterly.

'I sold. It was easy. The deals were normally agreed beforehand at a higher level: We took potatoes from the Hungarians, they took chemicals from us. They call that trade. Christ, we had more potatoes than we could eat anyhow, but the Hungarians had nothing else so we took them. I was only going through the motions all this time, shaking hands, signing pieces of paper. Early '65 I started to come West. In the beginning it was always with a delegation. Trade missions, they called them: strength in numbers. Only married men were allowed to go because they wouldn't abandon their families.' He smiled bitterly again.

'In those days we didn't actually sell anything at all. We weren't expected to. It was a long term penetration. That's the advantage of the system over there. They don't have balance sheets or annual profits. We were just preparing the ground, making ourselves known, proving that we didn't have horns growing out of our heads. The real horse trading would come later, maybe years later. Then Holmstangl in West Berlin did some sums and realised they could buy chemicals from us and undercut the whole Federal market. Our basic production costs were much lower and there were no import charges because the Federal government did not recognise East Germany and everything was treated as internal trade.

Somebody had to come over with samples to see if they met the Federal standards. That was me. I brought them in plastic containers and Holmstangl sent them up to the government laboratory in Hamburg. A couple of months later we got the all clear.'

Barnard wound his own window down and flipped the cigarette end out. He watched it glow briefly in the damp grass, then die.

'Atkins approached you?'

'Yes, but not at first. People were more careful then — there weren't so many coming across the checkpoints, and it would have been too easy to narrow it down to the few who were. In the end, early '66, Atkins just invited me out to lunch. I knew him quite well already. He didn't tell me lies.' He stared at Barnard. 'And he didn't threaten me.'

The jeep appeared again, drawing Barnard's eye. 'They are only armed with pistols,' he observed. 'Very strange.'

'They don't need anything else,' Gause said. 'The strip between the wire and the road is all mined. The pistols are only so that they can survey each other.' He paused until the jeep had gone. 'Atkins was very sympathetic. He was almost concerned for me. He asked me a lot of questions, about what sort of place I lived in, and how much I earned. In 1965, we weren't doing so well, either. The wall had not been up long and we were still sorting ourselves out after the exodus which had preceded it. 'Children's clothing' Atkins said. 'Is that hard to buy? Toys — toys at Christmas, how do you manage?' So I said that I wasn't paid much, but rents were low and food was cheap. But I asked him exactly what he was talking about.'

''I want you to run a delivery service for me,' he said, so quietly and earnestly that you would have thought he was asking me a personal favour. 'Only if you really want to, of course. Nothing dangerous at all; at least not if we are sensible. I will give you a box number in a post office in East Berlin,' he said. 'You just go along before you come over on one of your visits and collect what has been deposited there. Then bring it over. Sometimes, there won't be anything to bring, but you will be paid just the same. You won't even have to sign anything in the post office, all that has been taken care of.' He offered 200 marks a time. Later, he increased it to 250. Inflation, I suppose.'

Barnard was checking his watch, waiting for the jeep to come back. 'They're late,' he said flatly.

'They have probably stopped somewhere quiet for a cigarette. That's not unknown,' Gause replied. Just then it appeared. 'So I thought about the proposition. It was a lot of money, almost two months' wages. And all in West German marks. Listen, I'm not that innocent, I knew how hard it would be ever to get out once I was in, but it was still a lot of money. My only chance. So I agreed, as casually as I could, in a corridor at Holmstangl, as a matter of fact. He just nodded. He must have assumed I would agree.

'I was nervous at first. Going into a post office seemed so obvious, but nothing ever happened. From time to time, the post office was changed but

Atkins always warned me well in advance. The packets were small and I put them in the containers with the chemical samples. When I got to Holmstangl, I just handed them to Atkins.'

'You didn't know whose operation it was?'

'Not at first. I had imagined it was American — we imagine everything like that is. My English was not so good then and I couldn't tell an American from an Englishman. I can now, of course.'

'How did you find out?'

'Atkins. He told me one day. I thought it was funny. I almost laughed out loud. The British — really I hadn't anticipated that. The British are still around, but they don't seem to be doing much. Sorry if I offend you.'

'You never had any contact with anyone except Atkins?'

'Not until you today.'

Gause lit his pipe. The smoke curled away as he exhaled it, flattening itself against the windscreen.

'I'm sincerely sorry,' he said. 'If I knew who killed him, I would tell you. He was such an inoffensive man. Why don't you make a few enquiries in East Berlin? You must still have people there.'

'You ever visit his apartment?'

Gause shook his head. 'It was a business relationship we had, nothing more.'

'How come you speak such good English?' Barnard wondered.

'It is necessary to have a full command of the language in exports. Each summer, they send me on a special course, lectures, books, records, tapes, films, the whole works.' He was proud of the colloquial phrase. 'Do you speak German?'

'Enough.'

Gause looked at his watch.

'OK, we'll go now,' Barnard said.

'I need to cross by eight, otherwise the natives get restless.' It was the nearest he would come to making a joke, and Barnard had the grace to force something resembling a smile. 'There will have been something you have been wondering, because I am a stranger: Have I told you the truth? I do not tell lies. If you do, you never go to Heaven.'

'I won't be going to Heaven,' Barnard said.

He ran Gause back to Mariendorf, dropping him a few streets away from the Holmstangl offices. He drew the car up to the kerbside and again switched the lights off.

'I want to quit now, here and now,' Gause said. 'No more packets.'

'Just forget it ever happened. I'll only contact you if I want some more questions answering.'

'You won't make trouble for me?'

'I hope not. Give my regards to your wife.'

'That, I presume, is English humour.'

'Something like that.'

Gause was on the point of shaking hands. He changed his mind and opened the car door. 'I hope you find the man who did it, that's all,' he said.

'I will.'

★   ★   ★

Stenski returned to the office on the Friday. Without speaking to anybody, he began to sort through all his papers. He devised a system, because that was his way: Everything was divided into three heaps on the floor, the first to be passed on to the permanent appointment; the second to be dealt with before his departure; the third to be destroyed. He would retain nothing for himself.

By early afternoon, just as Johnson was coming back from Artur's Keller, he had finished. The heaps were substantial.

Stenski rang the commissionaire and asked him to come up. Together, they poured the last heap into a sack and went out across the courtyard to the small, brick building where the incinerator was housed. The commissionaire, a squat man always known as Sergeant Wilson, had difficulty igniting it. It was a huge, gun-metal grey thing with a mechanism hidden at one side for ignition. Wilson squatted down to examine it, and the fabric of his dark blue tunic was stretched so tightly against his wide body that it seemed it might split. At length, using a silver cigarette lighter, he did light it. Through the square opening, Stenski could see the flames rise. For a few moments there was a stale, unpleasant smell and, because the door to the building was still open, the wind drew out a little smoke. Stenski coughed. Wilson began dipping his hands into the sack, lifting out sheaves of papers and pushing them through the opening. They fell down and away: and the flames devoured them.

Stenski stood back and just watched.

To a sensitive man, it would have seemed a deep and very personal irony that everything should have come to this: An old man in an old coat, all but alone in a brick building full of the smell of ashes and the lingering odour of white-wash from the walls, watching the systematic destruction of what he had created. But he was concentrating on something else: That all the papers were properly destroyed.

Johnson came back to the Embassy later that evening. Stenski was still there, in the emptied room. Johnson had insisted that they go out for a farewell dinner. Now he wondered if that was a mistake. Stenski ate sparingly, and often neglected to eat at all. He took no interest in food and preferred sandwiches, because they did not demand the manipulation of cutlery and could be consumed while he was doing something else. He used to relate that, whenever the caretaker's wife at the apartment cooked for him in the evening — as a concession, he ate with them in their kitchen — she always gave him far too much. 'I have told her so many times that I cannot manage it all,' he said, 'but it's useless.'

Johnson could picture it all: Stenski sitting humbly at the table, the big woman standing with her back to the cooker; her husband, a tall, angular amateur cyclist who led his bicycle into the room so that it should be near him — as if he could draw warmth from it, as others do domestic animals — sitting in silence, thumbing through the evening newspaper.

But that Friday night, with a sea of beckoning neon light, Berlin was like a city discovering decadence and Johnson wanted to say goodbye to it — to the springs wandering through the Tiergarten, to the summers boating on the Havel, to the autumns in the Berliner Forest, even to the two winters of endless dampness and cold — in style. He knew he should have forgotten Stenski, found a girlfriend from somewhere, and done the thing properly; but that would have been wrong. He was closer to Stenski than he suspected.

Of course, Stenski protested. Stenski was exhausted, Stenski had far too much to do and Stenski did not care for dining out. Johnson was insistent. He lifted the telephone and ordered a taxi. That, somehow, settled it. They went down the Tiergarten, wide and ghostly with the high street lamps set back into the trees; circled the island where the war memorial stood, and moved towards the Brandenburg Gate, a colossal, lonely edifice supported by six columns and, looping in front of its base, the Wall: A flat, finite thing of breeze blocks, just too high to give a view of the Unter den Linden boulevard on the eastern side. Johnson glimpsed the concrete observation post to the left of the Gate, back from the Wall: An elongated pill-box on stilts with a narrow slit for vision running, like an open wound in the belly, across its front.

The taxi went no nearer than that. All traffic was directed off into Alt Moabit, and they passed into the shadows after the ethereal light of the white arc-lamps which illuminated the Wall from the eastern side. In Potsdamer Platz, they saw it again as it ran along to the canal then turned back on itself and went away in the centre of an area which had been cleared between the houses. On the other side, all the windows of the houses overlooking it had been crudely bricked up; on the western side, slogans had been scrawled. It was, as Stenski remarked, very odd. None of them were political, as if nobody cared any more.

They reached the Mehring Platz a few moments later and, just as Johnson had suspected, Stenski noticed the U-bahn station sign on the far side of it, and said, pointedly, that they should have used that.

The night club was called, for no

visible reason, the Arizona, an echo from the time when Berlin was full of American servicemen, and all things American were considered important. The main room was punctuated by ornate pillars with tables arranged to border the heart-shaped cabaret area, which also served as a dance floor. A cocktail bar was set into the back wall and a few girls sat on tall, ungainly stools in front of it, watching but not drinking.

They got a table in a corner. Stenski only wanted a steak — very well done, he insisted to the waiter, brown even in the middle. He had a horror of anything undercooked, even sausages. Johnson regarded the menu expansively, and having made a full choice, selected the wines like a man who knew what he was doing. He started with a bottle of Mosel from Bernkastel. Stenski drank sparingly, and approached a wine glass like a sparrow at a drinking bowl, hovering, then sipping quickly, in tight, nervous movements as if, in the very act of dipping his head, he could no longer see what was happening around him and was suddenly vulnerable. Johnson felt relaxed. He liked the Mosel with its soft, almost imperceptible nuances of the autumn days when the grapes were ripe.

'Feeling a little sad?' Johnson asked.

He would never have enquired about Stenski's sentiments without a couple of glasses inside him. Their relationship would not have permitted it. Stenski did not reply for some moments. He drank briefly from his glass. Then he said: 'I'm too old.' Johnson's first course arrived, a plate of sea food. 'I'm too old for the building and the re-building,' Stenski went on, monotone, when the waiter had gone. He seemed, very suddenly, an exhausted man, adrift. 'I must work for another seven years before I can retire.' It stretched before him, years already lost. 'I must consider my pension.' He had never mentioned it before. And by talking about it, he had drawn it closer still. 'That's why I put forward my idea when I was in London. I've nothing to forfeit except the pension.'

He hesitated for a moment. He was measuring his words against the occasion.

'They said some things in London . . . some kind things . . . but it's no good. I'm too old. I was walking this week and I came across a school playground. The children were enjoying themselves, running and screaming and laughing. That was when I first thought about it all very seriously: I said to myself, what am I doing? Am I protecting the children, doing our kind of work?' His hands were interlocked in front of him on the table. 'The children don't want what we try to give them. They don't want to go on fighting a thirty year old war. The Wall has no meaning for them. You saw the slogans. As far as they are concerned, it has been there forever. I know because I have enquired into these matters with the caretaker's nephew. 'The Wall? That's just too bad,' he says. 'Why worry about it so much?'

'I have also asked him about the German territories which were lost in the east. I mentioned names . . . names of towns now in Poland which have been changed: Elbing, Allenstein, Ortelsberg. He had never heard of them. That, of course, I could understand. It is hardly the point. He was not interested, he was absolutely indifferent.'

Johnson wiped his lips with the serviette and dropped it in a small heap on the table.

'There was a young girl in the playground, supervising the children,' Stenski said. 'She was a teacher, I suppose. She could not have been more than twenty. I kept thinking as I watched: I'm generations away from her. I'm a dinosaur. Extinct. Everything I know is only history to her. My father remembered the real Hapsburg Empire. He used to talk about the fine gold coaches and the state processions when that kind of thing wasn't tradition, it was reality.

'I contrast that girl with my own school days. It was a small village school, with only one master who always wore a black suit. It was a stone building, heated by a stove, and the books we used were old. They smelled of mildew. He taught us everything, history, mathematics, geography . . . and he believed in mastering the basics. He used to say that, in the world, a man is judged by his handwriting, his punctuation and his appearance.

'Do you know when the state processions went by, my father stood and saluted? Workmen came out of the fields to cheer. Women crossed themselves and blessed their rulers. How could I ever explain that to a girl of twenty, with her own car and money for good clothes and holidays, and probably living with a man?'

Johnson ate and listened, tugging at the shrimps to shell them and leaving the pink-tinged casings in a pile at the side of his plate.

'You know that normally I do not concern myself with ethical questions,' Stenski said. He needed to talk now. 'I leave that to London. We do our work, we are technicians not crusaders. When I told London what I had in mind, they really didn't understand it. I could sense it. I said: If you are going to run an intelligence service, you have to do dirty things from time to time, take a few risks, get some mud on your hands. If you don't run it that way, we might as well give up. But they don't evaluate like that in

London. They see it all in the abstract; what they claim is seeing the whole picture. They say: Something could go wrong, and the consequences would be this or that, the repercussions would be this or that. But I say: You can't measure it in those dimensions. It's not a financial transaction designed to look good on a balance sheet. I say: Look, I have an idea for an operation, and it's the kind of operation we have to do — because if we don't, we cease to exist. We might as well all be filing clerks, like those people in the records department. Do you understand?'

Johnson nodded. He had finished eating, and his plate was strewn with the wreckage of the seafood. A single dismembered claw lay alone near the shrimps. The Mosel was almost finished and Johnson motioned to pour some more, but Stenski declined, covering the top of his glass with his hand. A band had begun to play in the shadows, a procession of neutral trans-Atlantic melodies which gave neither pleasure nor pain.

'They kept me waiting,' Stenski said. 'I found the file I wanted, but you have to go to so many different clerks to get the right pieces of paper signed before you even ask somebody to get a file out. They have a new index system, coded and geared to a computer. They call that security. I didn't put the idea forward until I had seen the file, of course. I knew they would object initially, and I needed as much ammunition as I could get.

'I don't think they have ever liked me in London. You know, I'm a foreigner, even now. They are always' . . . and he reached out for the word, took his time finding it — 'condescending. Especially the ones who are well educated. At first, I thought it was because I was Jewish. We learn to watch for that. I only realised later on that it wasn't that, it wasn't that at all. It was because I'm just foreign.'

Johnson smiled. 'I can't believe it.'

'The English are so strange. You don't see it, of course. A Chinaman once said: 'Of all the people we have to negotiate with, the English are the most difficult. Nobody understands how they think.'

'The first time in my life that I met an Englishman was here in Berlin, a few months after the war. He was in a bar, the kind of place which had sprung up: A few barrels sawn in half for seats, sawdust on the floors, and whisky at big prices. It was full of Russian officers, and after a while, two Russian soldiers were delegated to go out and look for women. The Englishman sat by himself in a corner, drinking some kind of soda water. When three or four women were dragged in — one of them must have been over sixty and the other a pathetic fifteen year old — the officers began on them.

'The Englishman stood up very solemnly, produced a revolver and pointed it at the most senior of the Russian officers. He smiled. He motioned to the women and they ran away. Then he sat down again. The Russians all shook their heads and laughed at him. He continued drinking his soda water. I think that it was at the moment that I knew I wanted to work for the English.'

'What were you doing?'

'Serving behind the bar.'

'How did they recruit you?'

'It began in that bar. People wanted

things, and I made myself useful. I knew where things could be found — tooth-paste, shaving cream, cigarettes. They all used me, and I made a little money. They knew I'd been in the camps, because in the bar I worked with my sleeves rolled right up. They could see the number on my right arm, just above the elbow.'

'Is it still there?'

Stenski said nothing. 'It wasn't some-thing you traded on, and it wasn't something you tried to hide in those days. It was a fact of life, as unremarkable as a birthmark.' He paused, searching back down the years to the chaos which had engulfed Berlin. 'At first, I wasn't on the payroll, they paid me out of the petty cash. Later . . . later, they began to use me in sophisticated ways.'

The steaks came, and a bottle of Bordeaux, three years old. Johnson tasted it very seriously. 'Too young,' he said confidentially, 'but never mind.' The band stopped and three girls half-encased in ostrich feathers danced the can-can. Afterwards an announcer told some obscene jokes and then sang. They were far down the Bordeaux when the stripper came on, preceded by a roll of drums. It occurred to Johnson that Stenski was partially drunk, something he had never seen, or even imagined, before. He ordered brandies, and Stenski did not refuse. The stripper wore black, tight riding trousers and a black velvet hunting jacket and tried to look coy as she undressed. When she was completely naked, and the band were silent, she was uncertain what to do: Leave, or give them something stronger. The house lights had not been extinguished, as she might have expected. Vainly she sought the announcer for guidance, but he was not there. People began to laugh, and a voice called out for her to get on with it. She lost her nerve and fled, leaving the clothing where she had discarded it.

The girls at the bar had mostly found their customers now but one approached Johnson, a half caste more negro than white, wearing a short skirt and no nylons. He dismissed her hopeful look with a shake of the head. She shrugged and threaded her way back through the tables to the bar where she sat by herself. Nobody approached Stenski.

'You could have invited her to sit down,' Stenski said. 'I would not have minded.'

'Don't want to catch anything,' Johnson replied. The brandy came and Stenski sat back in his chair. 'Paul, you have somewhere to go back to, you belong somewhere,' he said very quietly. 'I have not been to the country where I was born since 1942. I will never go back now. I am not even permitted to do so. Nothing is left there. The only relative I know about is an aunt. I had a letter from her a long time ago. Probably she is dead now.'

Johnson remembered the bleak apartment which Stenski inhabited, overlooking the park; there were no photographs in it, no mementoes gathered over the years. Stenski could have packed and moved out at any time, given just a few minutes' warning.

'When I went to the mortuary to see Atkins' body, the attendant wanted me to be upset. He knew I was Jewish. Those people can smell it. But Paul, the days when I could be upset like that were long, long ago. I saw too much.' Johnson was sure the man was drunk now. 'You know what they used to say about us, the people who had been in the camps? Whatever happens to you afterwards, however long you live, a part of you will always be dead. You know why they said that? Because you can only stand so much suffering and then you don't care. You don't even care about the women and children. I wonder if that surprises you?

'They cried at night. That was terrible, and, Paul, I can hear it now, especially the children, always the children, the little lost ones, but I used to sleep right in the middle of them as if I was at home in bed. You would wake up in the night, you would see the torches and the guards would be in the room, picking people out — they had lists of the names, and they used to call them out — and when they had taken the quota away, everybody went straight back to sleep.'

He leant forward.

'That is how I came into this business. I never understood at the time why they took me on. I was just an ordinary camp survivor, and there were plenty about. It was dirty then, not like now. People had seen killing on a big scale, five solid years of it, so who could blame anybody for killing a bit more? But London knew something else. London knew that these people would go home soon, back to their nice little houses and be secretly repelled by what they had done. They would marry and have children and run grocery shops. But with my kind it would be different. London understood that. They knew that in another ten or twenty years, I would feel no repulsion.'

'Which camp was it, if I may ask?'

'Sorbibor.'

'How long were you there?'

'Three years. They took me on Christmas Eve, 1942. I remember that night for many reasons, but mainly because of the Christmas tree in the village square. Every year people laid presents under it, and the mayor came on Christmas morning and took them all to an orphanage. I remember looking at the tree before I got into the van. I don't remember the last instant I saw my mother.'

'Another drink?'

'No.' Stenski moved the empty glass from one place to another, seeking comfort from touching it. 'You know what I felt when I saw Atkins' body? Nothing. At least, nothing to speak about.'

*   *   *

Barnard had compiled a list. Gause had been the first name on it. A man called Sangster was second, but only because he had a reputation as a talker. Barnard rang him in Passports and invited him up to the office.

Sangster came, happy to find a diversion from his work. Sangster: goalkeeper for the Embassy hockey team, sporty, confident, the kind of Englishman who demonstrate why people don't like Englishmen. 'Anything I can do for you?' he asked blandly. But he watched

Barnard across the room. He had a deep contempt for the intelligence people. He regarded them as poseurs who never actually did a damn thing. Cowboys was his word.

'I just want a little background,' Barnard said. He was sitting at Stenski's desk, but there was nothing on it except the telephone.

'What background?'

'Atkins. Everybody seems to have known about him.'

'It was in the newspapers,' Sangster said. There was no mistaking the savouring of that fact. 'We've had some pretty classic cock-ups here over the years, I can tell you, but that kind of publicity was something else.'

'How many people knew about Atkins before that?'

'Plenty. We're only a little community here, he was British, and that alone made him a pretty rare bird. He came here occasionally and went over to Artur's Keller for a drink. He only touched fruit juice. Imagine that.' Sangster came further into the room. 'We weren't supposed to know what he was. But security here . . . '

'Wasn't it pretty insecure, coming for drinks?'

'If you really want my opinion, I don't think Stenski had a clue. We called him The Relic. He was like a throwback to the war. The thinking was decades out of date. And he lived like a hermit. God knows how Johnson stuck him so long.

'I organised the Christmas party three years running, and Stenski never came once. He pleaded the Jewish excuse at first, you know, not their Christmas. He didn't bother to reply to the invitations the second or third years. Foreign of course. Different mentality. No sense of corporate morale. Selfish, I should say. But hey, don't you run off thinking Atkins broadcasted what he did. He didn't write letters to The Times complaining about his working conditions. He was just a timid little perisher. Frightened to death of Stenski, eh? Shouldn't be surprised.

'Atkins had been around for a long time. Years. Much longer than most of the rest of us. The turnover in the Embassy can be pretty drastic. Most tours last four years, but plenty don't stick it out that long. The Germans get on their nerves, or the bloody constriction — whatever direction you set off in, you come up against the Wall. The East Germans have got dogs out there. Ever seen them? They're as big as pit ponies, and they tether them to stakes 50 yards apart with leads just so long that they can't attack each other. They're trained even to go for their handlers. A hell of a lot of normal British people can only take so much of that, particularly the ones with kids.

'You know West Berlin is entirely encircled by the Russians and we've only four old tanks here? It's not everybody's cup of tea.'

'I like dogs,' Barnard said.

That made Sangster laugh, an awful Public School laugh. 'They're not dogs, they're like wolves. My God, if Atkins had been walking one of those he wouldn't have got very far. Nobody would have had to do him in — the dog would have taken care of that. Had him for supper.' The thought amused him. 'What about you?' he said. 'Where did they find you?'

'I've been around,' Barnard replied.

'Always play hard-boiled Harry?'

He shrugged. 'What you think of me could hardly matter less.'

'Are you still going to be here at Christmas? It's only six or seven weeks away. I'd better get your name on the list for the party. I could always delete it later if anything happened to you.'

'I don't believe in Santa Claus.'

'Amazing. I'd never have guessed.'

\* \* \*

Johnson fastened his seat-belt at the last moment because he found them constricting and uncomfortable. Stenski had already fastened his and sat some distance up the aeroplane and on the other side of the gangway. The plane moved awkwardly away from the terminal building and taxied out along one of the slipways towards the runway: gained it and lumbered, elephantine, off into the distance, turned and waited fifteen minutes. Then it went all at once, its

69

engines given full power and pressing the passengers back against their seats; bounced along the runway, gathering momentum; shuddered at the instant of leaving the ground, seeming to dip as it rose and the wheels tucked themselves noisily into the belly. They were up.

Johnson saw the curved terminal building of Tempelhof fall away, and he had a sudden feeling of elation as they moved across the web of roads and houses far below, still climbing. He looked down carefully. They must have been over Steglitz, going out towards Lichterfelde; then Zehlendorf, then Schlachtensee; over the southern tip of the Havel, the wide expanse of water half seen and half lost in cloud; out across open country, now too high to see anything except the cloud which closed around them. The no-smoking signs went off abruptly. He turned from the window and looked up the plane towards Stenski. He was already asleep.

The journey to Vienna took a little under two hours. They were served with a miserable meal of cold meat and rolls, pre-wrapped in polythene. Stenski picked at it fitfully with his plastic cutlery, lost interest and sank back into sleep, his seat belt still fastened. He woke only for the descent.

Stenski insisted that they take the airport bus, and not a taxi. It was only nine kilometres and, being lunchtime, the traffic was light. He had already booked them in at a hotel called The Imperial, a five storey, grey, dignified building in Bahnhof Platz, directly opposite the railway station. They shared a room on the fourth floor, along an eternity of redcarpeted corridors and whispering, cage-like lifts. It was a large room, left over from the days when travellers expected spacious accommodation. They unpacked quickly, and Stenski went off without saying where.

Johnson wandered over to the station where there was a tourist office, and they gave him a street map. He walked for a couple of hours and, when darkness began to draw in and the offices empty, took refuge from the rush hour in a snack bar.

When Stenski came back, he said only: 'Nothing will happen this week, possibly not even next week. I will be very busy in the meantime.'

'If you don't want me around, I'll go and spend a few days on the ski slopes. There is a place in Austria where you can hire equipment and ski, even at this time of year,' Johnson said.

In the morning, he left by train for Schladming.

★   ★   ★

Winter had brought a cleansing to Berlin. The shifting layers of mist still hung low over the Havel at night, but the dampness had gone and, from early evening until dawn, frost came down like a frozen skin. Barnard didn't mind that because it was better for his chest; the dampness was not, and he coughed wretchedly every morning when he woke in autumn. He'd been a heavy smoker for almost all his life, and he'd always liked a drink too. 'I've got all the vices except one,' he would say as a conversational point. 'I'm not queer. That's the only one I haven't got.'

He was 43 and looked slightly older. Never married. He'd joined the Army at 17, the week after he left school, and a certain flavour of the military remained with him: He held himself erect, even when sitting down, and tucked his handkerchief into his jacket sleeve at the wrist; he liked his hair short — almost a regulation cut — and kept himself fit. One of his hobbies had been weapons, particularly small arms; and he had been trained in other ways, with an emphasis on hand-to-hand combat. He had remembered all the principles, the pivots and counter-pivots; and people, sensing what he was, tended to stay away from him. He had always found small talk difficult, and that had heightened his sense of isolation. Only the military mentality could he comprehend, or could comprehend him.

London had been specific. He had been briefed by a man called McClellan — one of those deceptive people in wellcut suits with a smooth and polished personality who, in fact, come from tough towns in Scotland and acquire the sophistication along the way — who had given him a series of detailed instructions.

The office was near the Mall, overlooking the RAC club. Through the curtained windows, Barnard could see the cars and taxi cabs struggling up towards the roundabout in front of Buckingham Palace.

'Let the local police make their enquiries about Atkins. There will be an inquest, no doubt. Steer clear of it. Assuming that they find nothing, and it is reasonable to assume that they will not, we will ask, quite openly and through the Embassy in Berlin, for permission for one of our men to look into it. We have every right. Atkins was a British subject, as British as you or I. The local police will therefore be obliged to grant our request.'

McClellan was younger than Barnard. He had some kind of dossier before him, which he glanced at from time to time. It was closely typed, in single spacing. 'But you go carefully,' he said. His voice had changed. 'Don't rush it. Be circumspect.

Don't go kicking people in the groin, just because they happen to get in your way.'

★   ★   ★

The factory was at the back of a new industrial estate. Buildings were grouped along a central avenue with delivery vans in the loading bays. Holmstangl comprised three buildings, with a red sign across the top of the taller, central one proclaiming their name. The ranks of windows were all tinted smoke-grey and the low, heatless morning sun shimmered against them.

Barnard found the export department on the third floor. The deputy head buyer agreed to meet him, and he was ushered into a plain office and offered a seat. From the window, he could see the Volkspark, with a playing area to its left, flanked by trees, and three football pitches, their goalmouths worn bare of grass.

The deputy head buyer came in after a few moments, an elderly man. 'I'm from the British Embassy,' Barnard said as they shook hands. 'I am afraid your police have not had much success looking into what happened to Mr. Atkins. Since we have a direct interest in this, we are making some enquiries of our own.'

'You will please understand how much one regrets this terrible matter.' The head buyer spoke stiff, taught English. 'It was not only that Mr. Atkins was a colleague of us, but that he had such a happy personality. He was most popular, hard working and punctual in all works he undertook. His office was close to this one.'

'I must ask you some questions.'

'Please.'

'Did he have any close friends?'

'I believe it was not so. He lived alone, but he did not discuss his home life — that is the correct phrase, yes?' Barnard nodded, and the man smiled with obvious pleasure. 'Perhaps it is not the same thing in England, but here in Germany we work long hours and do not find our friends at the office. We are pleased not to see them any more at the end of the day. Therefore although Mr.

Atkins and I are knowing each other for several years, I never had the occasion to visit his home.'

'Did he ever seem worried about anything?'

'No, no. You did not have the occasion to meet him? Such a pity. He was what I call an optimist man. Even on the most rainy afternoon, he retained his happy face.'

'Girl friend?'

'I had never thought of it. Permit me, I will ask. It is not so indiscreet.' He flipped a switch on the intercom and asked somebody the question in German. 'My secretary, who is also knowing him well, says she never heard of any girl friend. She adds that she thinks it most improbable. He was not such a young man.'

'You don't have to be tactful,' Barnard said. He lit a cigarette, and the man came politely over with an ashtray, the name Holmstangl written in the same styled red lettering around its rim and, immediately after that, a slogan: Chemicals you can trust. He placed it awkwardly on the carpet between his feet.

'What about hobbies? What did he do at the weekends?'

'I have no idea. He never spoke about it — except golf.' He flipped the intercom switch again. 'Yes, it is confirmed. He played golf. Very British. I will discover, if you wish, the name of the place where he played.' He went away, leaving the door ajar, and returned a few minutes after, holding a piece of paper torn from a shorthand notebook. He handed it to Barnard. 'This is the address. You will please give this to your taxi driver, and thus he will be enabled to take you there without difficulties.'

'What about his apartment?'

'It is over there.' They went to the window together. 'You see the trees,' and he pointed. 'It is behind them. You can walk there if you wish. Have you the number of the apartment? Good. I can see that you are a man well prepared. I will point to you the direction.'

They went down in the lift and out into the concrete yard full of stacked cardboard boxes, then through a gate. They shook hands again and Barnard walked between two of the football pitches towards the trees. There was hoar frost, white and crisp, in a retreating line where the trees had shielded it from the sun. As he reached the path in the trees, he turned and saw his footprints preserved in it. He followed the path.

The apartment blocks were futuristic in design, all different in shape, with angled roofs: some constructed on stilts. The gardens had been landscaped with lawns and monkey puzzle trees. To his left, in a clearing, he could see a hard tennis court and, beside it, a small ornamental lake spanned by a mock Chinese bridge. A minute island in the middle was covered by a rockery. Ice lay across the water.

He looked at the houses again. They were made of red bricks, and they might almost have been artificial. All the windows were wide, and of a single pane. Most had been hung with lace curtains. This little lot must have set Atkins back a bit, Barnard thought. Forget the ideology, he was in it for the same reason as Gause: To pay the rent on his dreams.

The number was 73, in a larger block than the rest. The door was closed. He rang the bell and an old man in uniform came. His shirt was buttoned right up, but he wore no tie. A woman with an apron, secured round her waist by a length of blue cord, peered over his shoulder.

'Yes?' the old man said.

'I've come about one of your tenants, a Mr. Atkins. I work for the British Embassy.'

'He's dead,' the man said, without opening the door fully.

'That's why I have come.'

The door was eased reluctantly back and the woman retreated; but she didn't go too far away, and she wasn't going to miss anything.

'Just a few questions,' Barnard said.

'I don't know about that. I'm the caretaker, and the police said not to tell anybody anything.'

'I understand that.' The German was coming back to him fast. 'But it concerns his relatives in Great Britain. They are very upset and the Embassy has promised to help. We need to know how much clothing and furniture he had. All that may have to be shipped back.'

'It's not my fault,' the caretaker said. 'I only do what I'm told.' The Nuremburg defence: Acting under orders. Mindless bastards, Barnard thought. The man must have been seventy, a thinned, bird-like creature who had shrunk with age and was now a size too small for the uniform. He wore brown shoes which looked hopelessly wrong with the navy blue jacket and trousers. 'The police said not to say anything to anybody.'

'I have been given full permission by the police. It's only a few questions,' Barnard said. 'Nothing too painful. What happened on the night Atkins died?'

'I've told the police . . . '

'Now tell me.'

'It was about ten o'clock. Herr Atkins came for our dog. We've a dog but I can't walk it in the winter because of the cold and my wife's legs are bad. He used to come most nights and we gave him the lead. He used to take the dog round the Volkspark.'

'He never wore a coat,' the woman said. She was still hovering. 'I told him about that, but he never would wear one. Some nights, he would come back frozen, hands in his pockets and his face red with the cold.'

'That night,' the caretaker said, 'the dog came back by itself. I heard it scratching the door and when I got there I saw it still had its lead on. I waited for a while, then I went out to look for him myself.'

'You didn't see anybody else?'

'No. It was too cold for other people to be out.'

'He was a model,' the woman volunteered, 'I wish there were more like that. Some of them make so much noise, and they have parties which go on right through the night. Never a thought for others trying to sleep. He was different.'

'Did he have a girl friend?'

'No.' It was she who was answering now. 'He was too nice for that. He wasn't like the other single men. He was decent. Sometimes, he would have his radio on, but quietly. He considered other people.

He used to listen to the English broadcasts. That is how we knew that it was his radio which was on.' She moved forward again so she was standing almost next to the caretaker. 'He used the other door because he walked home from work from that direction, from Holmstangl. We hardly ever heard him come in. Then, at half past nine every night, he knocked on our door and took the dog out. He loved the dog.'

'He bought the new lead for it,' the caretaker added.

'A good one. Real leather,' she said.

'He played golf?' Barnard asked.

'Yes,' she said. 'Every Wednesday afternoon. He had a car — it's still in the garage over there. I don't know what we are supposed to do with it. He kept his golf clubs in the boot. That's what reminded me of the car. They must be still there. He used to have dinner at the club, I think.'

'I'd better see his apartment,' Barnard said decisively. 'There is the question of an inventory.'

'The owners were wondering about

that,' the caretaker said. 'They can't re-let it until everything has been taken out. I think they were going to store it all somewhere, but the police didn't give them permission to move any of it.'

They went up the staircase to a landing on the first floor. The door to the right had number 73 screwed onto it, and a glass spy-hole for examining visitors from the inside. The caretaker had a big bunch of keys held by a chain to his trouser belt.

'It's not only these apartments we've to look after,' he said, 'We've another twenty.'

He sifted through the keys, found the right one and opened the door. Barnard went in alone while they stood outside, uncertain whether to follow. The hallway was very small, with a row of metal pegs along the wall behind the door, but no coat on them. He moved into the lounge, a square room with a large window giving a panoramic view of the lawns and the ornamental pond. The sun had reached it now, and the ice had melted back from the island.

Atkins had no taste. The furniture was

traditional and ill-suited to a modern apartment: An oak dining table against a wall by the window, a mahogany side-board, a leather armchair and sofa. Framed photographs stood on a shelf near the serving hatch from the kitchen. He went closer and examined them. None were of Atkins himself. One was of a girl in dark formal gown on graduation day; another, a baby in a carrycot; a third, a faded picture of a soldier in the desert with arid rocks behind him, and a little scrub land, creased as if it had been carried in a wallet for many years: A tall man, holding a beret in his left hand and grinning a boyish grin. It was signed in the bottom right hand corner: Good luck mate, Jimmy.

Barnard went into the kitchen. The fridge was full of tall, clear plastic containers holding fruit juice.

He wandered into the bedroom. The bed was made. Suits hung limp in the wardrobe, with five pairs of shoes spread out at its base. One pair had mud on the heels. He must have worn them one night when he was walking the dog. The rest had been cleaned.

Atkins, a neat, cautious man, clean and careful. Nothing was out of place; there was no nuance of human chaos.

Barnard stooped and opened a drawer of the writing desk, placed at a distance from the bed. It was strange to have it there, but perhaps there had been not enough space in the lounge. Papers were stacked in the drawer, bills, receipts, a letter or two from his cousin. That would be the girl in the graduation photograph. Very pretty. The child in the other photograph would probably be hers. The ascending scale of a life, school, university, marriage, a child, perfunctory divorce; the seeping tide of disenchantment. The other man, older, hardly wiser, but with money. An uneasy compromise with what they call reality, and forgotten dreams which would never come true. A residue of loneliness, and a measure of self-knowledge purchased from the ascending scale.

I bet Atkins never forgot the kid's birthday, Barnard thought. I bet he sent something extra special over at Christmas, something a damn sight more expensive than she could afford.

He left the room. The caretaker was still on the landing, but his wife had gone.

'Thanks,' Barnard said. 'There'll be no trouble.'

He walked back across the Volkspark, round the other side this time, away from the playing fields. Atkins had been killed near here, in the bushes. But there were too many bushes, and he couldn't deduce where it happened. It was not important, certainly not this length of time afterwards. Nothing would remain. The nightly dew would have cleansed the long grass.

Everybody loved Atkins, he told himself. The contact, the company, even the caretaker. Everybody except somebody.

★   ★   ★

In the afternoon he drove to the golf club.

The British had created it. It was they who had selected the site, on the edge of the Berliner Forest, which resembled, as

87

much as anything could, the Wiltshire Downs; it was they who had ordained the architect to design a British edifice of a clubhouse, granite blocks and ivy climbing up tall windows; and it was they who had commanded that turf lawns be brought, and flowerbeds, and evergreen bushes which never grew beyond waist high. Barnard entered through a back door. The main room was long and wide. At one end, a glass cabinet had been set back into the wall with silver cups in it; at the other, another case containing golf antiquities, ancient putters, a tattered pair of shoes, a scorecard signed by somebody. Every religion must have its holy relics.

He asked at the bar where the secretary's office was. The barman directed him away to a room where the secretary worked. It was more like a lumber room. Heaps of magazines had been piled against a wall. On the desk lay stratas of unanswered correspondence. The secretary, a stiff, unbending man in a dark suit, looked perpetually harrassed.

'Atkins? Oh yes, the little Englishman. There used to be so many of them. Not now. They've drifted away.' He spoke quickly, as if he wanted to finish every sentence before the telephone rang to interrupt him. 'Ten years ago you could walk into that main room and hardly hear German spoken. We even had an Irish barman. Now we have cultivated an international membership, mostly businessmen. They can hire clubs and have a few rounds. Plenty of Germans, too. You might think golf would not appeal to them, but ... I can show you the membership list. You would be surprised.'

'I'll take your word for it.'

The secretary stayed within reach of the telephone.

'You can have no idea what it's like here,' he said. 'It continues all day. I have to handle all the subscriptions, all the accounts, organise all the competitions. I even order the drinks for the bar. Now where were we? Ah, Atkins. He was a member for several years.' He stood up, moved to the bureau and consulted a black ledger. 'Nine years. I had no idea it was so long. He always paid his subscription by banker's order so I never saw much of him. He wasn't a very good golfer, I'm afraid. He never won anything, not even novice prize. He played at a certain level. Let us call it a social level. There are many like that. They do not have regular partners. They know a lot of other people who are about the same standard as themselves, and they organise to play each other.'

'Can you give me the names of people in that group?'

'It would be better to ask Claus. He works behind the bar. He knows things like that.'

The telephone did ring, and he seized it with a reflex action. Barnard stood up and the secretary motioned farewell still talking on the telephone.

Claus was almost completely bald. 'That little creep,' he said. 'Sure I remember him. Who could forget Atkins? It was always a Wednesday when he came. He drank fruit juice, fresh fruit juice, orange, grapefruit, tomato, stuff like that. He'd stand there with his friends and insist on buying them drinks, big whiskies, not much water, and have a godforsaken tomato juice for himself. I never saw him play golf. He waddled. But he was pretty damn particular. 'Claus' he said to me, 'a bigger measure of whisky than that for my friend. Claus, you can do better than that. Fill it up.' If I stared at him, he'd laugh nervously, and try to make a joke out of the complaint. Are all the English like that? I'm glad I've never been there.'

'These partners he had — were they close friends?'

'You ever meet Atkins? Nobody got close to a creep like that, nobody on God's earth. Nobody wanted to. He was false. I can tell. I'm famous as a judge of character. I never make mistakes. That's part of being a barman. You learn to read people fast. He was just a shallow little jerk. So what were you looking for, anyway: A goddam saint?'

'I'm looking for the man who killed him,' Barnard said evenly.

'That's right, little Atkins got killed. Hey, that's damn near a real joke. Who the hell would have wasted their time on him?'

'I'd like to know.'

'Sure you would. Hey — another thing. He used to come here with a woman, for dinner. He never brought her during the day. He took damn care she never saw him play golf.'

'Keep talking.'

'Sure, that's my life, talking. I never stop. Hadn't you noticed? I go on right up to the moment when they close this stinking place down every night. I talk four languages, maybe five. I forget. Want a drink?'

Barnard took a beer and made a mess of pouring it. The froth rose up inside the glass, swelled over the rim and cascaded down the outside. The barman lifted it and wiped the counter with a cloth.

'Hey,' he announced loudly. 'The English don't even know how to pour a beer anymore. Cheers.' He drank himself, from a glass secreted below the counter. Barnard tilted his glass back towards his mouth but got only froth, a taste he strongly disliked.

'Tell me about the woman.'

'Sure. Atkins had a woman, Atkins had

a woman. It's kind of hard to believe, a creep like that with a fat little stomach and a tame little saloon car. I nearly forgot the moustache.' It was curious, Barnard thought: Whenever anybody spoke of Atkins, it was always in the diminutive sense. 'OK, so maybe he had some money, but no broad is going to climb into bed with somebody like that just for money. She was quite presentable. Middle-thirties, been through the wringer. I can always tell. Hard as that.' He rapped his knuckles on the counter. 'Too much make-up, that's what gives the game away. She was an artificial blonde, like a dry haystack. He only brought her to show her off.'

'What was her name?'

'Christ knows.'

'Think anybody here would?'

'Maybe, I'll ask.'

Barnard took out a 50 mark note and handed it across for the beer. 'Keep the change.'

The barman went through a door into the kitchen, came back. 'Nothing. Even the waitresses don't remember. Hey Big

John,' he called out, and one of the members sitting with two other men at a table looked round. 'What was the name of that broad Atkins used to bring over here, the blonde one?'

'No idea. He never mentioned her name. He used to call her . . . What was it? Some pet name . . . my duchess, my princess. Something stupid like that.'

'Somebody must have known,' Barnard said. 'If not that, where she worked, where she lived. Something. That's all I want.'

'Sorry,' the man said. 'If she had been better looking we might have been more interested.'

The barman said: 'What did I tell you? A broad, that's what she was. Everybody thought the same.'

But Barnard was indifferent to that. 'If she wasn't a member, Atkins must have signed her in every time he came.' He returned to the secretary's office. The man was on the telephone again, a half-finished cup of coffee on the desk before him, the spoon still in it. Barnard stood by the door until he had finished talking.

'Atkins came here with a woman,' Barnard said as the secretary put the telephone down. 'He dined regularly with her. But nobody out there knew her name. That doesn't matter, because he must have signed her in as a guest.'

'No doubt,' the secretary said. 'He was always very proper. I would like to help, but really I have so much to do. You have seen yourself that the telephone rings all the time. It might take many hours of searching to find. My assistant is away . . . '

'Find it.'

'Young man, you came here this morning barking questions at me about a member — it was most unethical of me even to discuss a member. Now you demand that I cease all my work and spend what must be a considerable time . . . '

'Don't give me that. If you don't, I guarantee that within half an hour, I'll have half the Berlin police force up here looking for it. We'll see whether that little lot interrupts your work or not. Now get your ledger out and have a look. Find it.'

'I must ask you to leave this clubhouse, to which you have not been invited and to which, I assure you, you will not be invited.' He was caught between obedience and defiance. 'I will not surrender to crude threats.'

'It'll be nice publicity, especially when the British Embassy want to know why a German wouldn't help. Nice for you. But please yourself. I couldn't give a damn. The police will be much more thorough than me. Don't forget that. They'll want to talk to every member, go through all your drawers.' He paused, measuring the effect. 'It'll be a bloody sight bigger event than any golf tournament you've ever had.'

'You don't understand.' The tone of his voice had changed and lowered, moving back from anger to reason. 'The book is still out there at the reception desk.'

'So get it.'

'I protest: I protest at you, and at your attitude. In short, your whole conduct. You come barging . . . '

'Get it.'

He went away and returned with the

ledger, which he laid on his desk, a thick, green book with two columns ruled on each page, headed Guest's Signature and Member's Signature. A red ribbon, stitched to the spine of the book, was used to mark the current page. The secretary adjusted his spectacles and began to trace back down the columns with the index finger of his right hand. 'If only we had a date,' he murmered,' it would be infinitely simplified.'

Barnard had moved behind him and watched over his shoulder. The pages were crisp, the best paper.

It took ten minutes to find. 'Some of these signatures are in hand-writing which is most slovenly', the secretary observed with distaste. 'One can barely decipher them.'

He stood upright. 'Here it is. Mr. Atkins. That is how he must have styled himself.' Oh God, thought Barnard. Mr. Atkins. It stood out on the page, like a bowler hat among bald people. 'Member's signature, Eva . . . Eva something I cannot make out. You look if you wish.'

Barnard leant over the book and saw

the neat writing of Atkins. The woman must have written her name herself. The character of the hand-writing was quite different. Eva Karow. It looked like Karow, but the r was indistinct.

'It's Karow,' he announced to the secretary.

'Quite possible.'

'If that is her real name.'

For a moment, the secretary seemed slightly shocked. 'Why should it not be?' he asked plaintively.

That was the last day of November.

# Part Three

# The December Kill

Johnson liked ski-ing because it was possible, and desirable, to ski alone. He did not think of himself as a lonely man, but the nature of his work precluded casual friendships and living in the orbit of Stenski, who had no friends at all, seemed to isolate him.

He spent a long, careless week at Schladming, and Berlin seemed utterly remote. He travelled to the summit of Dachstein on an old ski lift with the rugged, sloping rockface falling away a hundred feet below him; drank hot coffee in a hut near the top where ski-ers went, clogging the place with hats and gloves, skis and ski poles; then skied down the far side, out into the sun, following a path down frozen gullies and across level expanses of snow, slithering back into the white canyons which took him into the pine trees; and in the trees there was a complete, cemetery silence except for the whisper of his skis and, sometimes, the flutter of caked snow falling from dry branches.

On the Friday, he came back to his hotel to change for lunch, and the woman who ran it said there had been a telephone call for him from Vienna. The caller wouldn't leave his name but said Johnson would know who it was. He rang from his room, and Stenski answered immediately. 'When,' he asked without formalities, 'is the next train back here?'

'I don't know.'

'You should have checked when you first arrived there.'

'There will be one tomorrow morning, I should think. Maybe tonight. But I have to get a taxi all the way to Innsbruck.'

'Come back tonight if you can.'

Johnson rang the railway station. There was a train at five, change at Salzburg.

He was thankful for the train journey. It gave him a last chance to rationalise his thoughts before he saw Stenski again. And Johnson, who could be very pragmatic, was deeply disturbed by what Stenski wanted to do. In wartime, in a confused situation, it might have worked, but not now, Johnson thought, not now. The whole concept was untypical of Stenski. Why had he suddenly abandoned caution and dreamed up something so absurd? That worried Johnson. And why had London agreed? McClellan was pragmatic, too; and even McClellan lacked the authority to have approved it. He would have had to seek that from higher levels. Yet — they had all approved it.

When Johnson got off the train shortly before midnight, he didn't know what to think. He walked across the square to the hotel. Stenski reached up a bony arm and switched on the bedside light. He wore plain lime green pyjamas, the buttons on the jacket done up to his neck.

'Paul,' Stenski said softly, 'everything has gone well. He is coming . . . '

'He?'

'He is called Alexis Andrushenko, and he works for Markov. He has a position of trust, otherwise they would never let him out. He would constitute a most valuable catch. He comes here regularly once a month. It is almost a joke in diplomatic circles. They call him The Period.'

Johnson took off his coat and began to unpack. 'When does he arrive next?'

'On Tuesday morning. Our people here have been quite magnificent. They have helped me in every way. I even have his flight number.'

Johnson said nothing. He went to the wardrobe, took some metal coat hangers from it and mechanically began to drape his suits over them.

'It all makes sense,' Stenski went on. There was no suggestion of intoxication at this preliminary success; just an even, dry voice explaining the position at a briefing. 'Andrushenko comes here and their people report to him personally. The Russians don't trust people; they like to hear it all for themselves. They believe middle men — even their own middle men — will cheat them.

'So Andrushenko installs himself within the Russian Embassy and they go to him there. Perhaps he is harsh with them. He sounds the kind. He was at the front during the war, after a time in Leningrad.

They gave him medals. The rumour is that he did some unpleasant things to German prisoners. Apparently he enjoyed hurting people.'

Johnson went to wash and Stenski talked on.

'Vienna is just the right place. Austria is a neutral country. It is — central. In one day, you can reach here from the Federal Republic, East Germany, Czechoslovakia, Hungary, Yugoslavia, Italy, Switzerland. That is why they selected it, no doubt.' He paused fractionally. 'Nobody could keep track of who came, or from where. You know what the customs are like these days. They just wave you through.' Johnson returned, drying the back of his neck with a towel, and stood framed in the bathroom door. Stenski looked up towards him. 'Andrushenko travels by aeroplane. He is met at the airport by an Embassy car. He is driven directly to the Embassy. Invariably he remains inside for three or four days. He is then driven back to the airport.'

'So you'll never get near him.' Johnson observed. He held the towel in his left hand like a club. 'What are you going to do: Hijack his car?' He went to the window and parted the curtains. The trees in the square were all bare, naked sentries guarding nothing. The wind had carried the leaves away. Now it tugged and pulled a discarded page of a newspaper along, half in the gutter. The traffic lights far away changed to green, releasing a handful of cars and a van. 'I've had time to think while I've been away,' he said, 'and I cannot understand why London agreed to all this. It's not their style, and it's not your style.'

'Paul,' Stenski said, 'you know why I went to London?'

'To look at an old file.'

'It was Andrushenko's file. I remembered him from years ago. Nothing changes. He was in East Berlin for a while. There was some trouble, but I couldn't remember what. It was bad enough for him to be sent home. We used to hear all the gossip like that before the Wall went up. I had forgotten about him until a year ago. Somebody mentioned that he was on the Vienna run.'

'So what?'

'It was all in the file, you see, the details of what he had been sent home for. I imagined it would be. People were very thorough then, and they wrote that kind of thing down for future reference. No good doing that now. Those clerks down there would throw it away.'

'Wonderful,' Johnson said bleakly. He let the curtains fall back together. 'Simply wonderbar.'

'I will tell you what he was sent home for: A sexual offence. Several sexual offences, as a matter of record. His tastes are not quite normal.'

'Men or women?'

'Women but . . . '

'He liked women. That is hardly an indictable crime.'

'They were East German women. The Russians were playing Fairy Godmother at that time, showing their new comrades the correct path forward. One of their people behaving like that was not quite what they wanted. Apparently Andrushenko took them right off the street; offered them lifts, then drove them out into the country. He nearly killed one woman. They had to take her to hospital. It was the hospital who filed an official complaint.' Stenski sat up, as if the whole force of the possibilities he had opened up had seized him. 'We are going to find him something he can't resist.'

'He might have changed. He must be fifty now, probably older. He could be a loving grandfather, with grandchildren bouncing on his knee.'

Stenski opened his mouth just wide enough for the single gold-capped tooth to be visible. 'I've told you: Nothing changes.'

★   ★   ★

The wind was constant. It was the wind of winter, friendless and unloved, cutting at the ranks of faces which waited, while the strands of darkness were drawn down upon the city, at cheerless bus stations, the paving stones damp underfoot. Johnson had not expected this. Vienna was an industrial city. Even the name evoked something else: Vast, ornate buildings; white horses moving in formation without a word of command; ballrooms full of beautiful people waltzing to Strauss; cobbled courtyards thick with the smell of freshly-ground coffee; mountains of cream cakes in old bow windows. He felt obscurely cheated.

When he woke, Stenski had gone. He walked that morning, and spent most of the afternoon in a public library, like a tramp, because it was warm.

Stenski came back at nine in the evening. 'We are leaving the hotel now,' he announced. 'The car is downstairs.'

'A car? Very civilised.'

'They have been very good to me.'

Stenski had little and he thrust it carelessly into his old leather suitcase; put on his hat and overcoat. His shoes were always perfectly clean. Johnson had always been intrigued by that and had speculated, when he first arrived in Berlin, that Stenski must carry a small cloth in a pocket and, when nobody was looking, run it across them to restore the sheen.

The car was a Mercedes, which

impressed Johnson further. The driver wore a dark suit and did not speak. The back of his neck was covered in small craters, the dried up marks of boils years ago.

They went north, through the suburbs. The open country took a long time to reach. They drifted through villages, and the headlights picked out the brightly-painted facades of the cottages. After that, they began to climb and the engine laboured. They turned off the main road and travelled seven or eight kilometres through three more villages, then another four kilometres along an unkept country lane. The house was half-hidden among conifer trees. Stenski had a key for the front door. When they were inside the narrow hallway, Johnson said: 'Where did you find this place?'

'There is an agency in Vienna which caters for businessmen with families who want to rent houses for short periods. I had to put a deposit down, in case we break anything.'

The driver brought the suitcases.

'Whose name is it in?' Johnson asked.

'I gave them a name from the past, a Czech cabinet minister who died before the war. That seemed the most secure way.' He motioned for the driver to take the suitcases upstairs. 'They were deplorably casual at this agency. They did not ask to see any identification papers. They only wanted one months' rent in advance, plus the deposit.'

The driver came down, and Stenski told him to go.

'Did you speak to them in Czech?' Johnson asked.

'Partly. Some very broken German.'

There were two bedrooms, and they took one each. The house must have been unoccupied for some time because it smelt stale. Johnson found the central heating unit and switched it on, but the thermostat was located somewhere else, and he couldn't find that. They spent a cold night.

He woke to a magnificent dawn flooding across the sky. He went to the window. The view of the valley was superb. Far away he could see houses grouped at the end of an arched, stone bridge which spanned the river, and, where the hills began to rise on the other side of the valley, a farm.

Stenski was still asleep, sniffling solemnly.

Johnson went down, but the fridge was empty. He discovered some tinned food and a jar of coffee in a cupboard and fashioned a meal.

'I'm sorry,' Stenski said when he had washed and dressed, and was sitting at the table in the kitchen. 'I never thought about food.' Johnson disliked coffee without milk, and drank it only to moisten his mouth. He still felt cold, the cold which lingers from the dawn and reaches into the bones.

Stenski finished eating. The sun was up now, above the distant hills, heatless and offering Johnson no comfort. 'It is time to go to the garage.' Stenski said. 'Leave the washing-up until later.'

When they were outside the house, Johnson turned to survey it: A square, brick building, each of the four front windows masked by white lace curtains. It was exactly the kind of homely, neutral architecture an agency would select. In front of it, the lawn ran away to a fence which bordered a newly ploughed field. The garden required no maintenance except a lawn-mower.

The garage was twenty yards away, a double garage of the same brick. Ivy grew along the wall which faced them, its leaves stirring in the breeze. The doors had been painted blue: Quite the wrong colour, Johnson thought, as they walked toward them. Again Stenski had the key, and he slid back one of the doors. The runners resisted at first, and it required a shove from the shoulder to make it move. The garage was empty, except for a heap of browning leaves which had been brushed into a far corner and, in the centre, a coffin laid on the concrete floor. The lid was on, but not screwed down.

Stenski walked over to it. 'The size is correct.' His voice carried an echo. 'They are manufactured in different sizes. This one is medium. I wonder if you knew that?'

Johnson joined him. The lid protruded by an inch all round. 'The holes are under it,' Stenski said. Johnson crouched and saw them, at intervals of three inches, bored into the woodwork. Neat little holes, made by an expert.

* * *

When they were back in the house, Stenski said 'Today we are going to check everything, each scrap of paper, each passport, each visa. You can have no conception of how much paper work is involved in this. It is almost infinite.'

'There is something I want to say,' Johnson began. 'I tried to say it when I came back from Schladming — but somehow the moment went away.' Both he and Stenski stood, as if they were in somebody else's house, and would have to be invited to sit down. 'There is something I need to say. I don't like what we're doing. I find the whole concept repugnant. More than that, I don't think it has a cat in hell's chance of working. If we make a mistake — if something unforeseen happens, if one stupid little detail trips us up — look, we've worked together for two years, we've done some things, some good things, but this one is crazy. It amounts to crude blackmail, abduction. It violates every standard of conduct which we are supposed to represent.'

Stenski was by the window, surveying the valley. 'Stalin was a great man because he fought barbarism with barbarism. Khrushchev said that.'

'Is that justification for an operation like this? Dear God, we've all gone crazy together. Listen — just listen to me for a moment. I agree with your sentiments about not sitting back and letting them come at us the whole time. But this is not the only alternative, a clumsy kidnap, a coffin with holes in it, a story so infantile that even the stupidest Austrian airport official will see through it.'

'Whether you are offended or not I cannot help,' Stenski said. 'I am not the guardian of your sensibilities, and I have no wish to be.' He sat down in one of the chairs and rested his hands on the thin arms. 'What will happen if Markov is allowed to continue? What took place in

Berlin will be repeated elsewhere. In case you have forgotten, we are vulnerable right across the map: Norway, Denmark . . . '

'I know that,' Johnson said. 'But, with you, it's something personal. It's you and Markov. You don't give a damn about the Norwegians. I bet you've never even been to Norway. You only want to damage Markov because he has damaged you.'

Stenski was not upset. 'You can go away if you want. Just ring for the Mercedes. I will give you the number.'

'That is an insult to me.'

Stenski shrugged. 'You don't seem to want to stay.'

'The operation won't work! It is transparent!'

Stenski stood up. 'You are incorrect,' he said. 'It will work because people are stupid and people are apathetic. They don't want inconvenience. It will work because it is unusual. Nobody, not even Markov, will be anticipating anything like it. That is the quality which appealed to London. Remember that I evaluate the risks as you do. I see them before they happen.'

'You really believe that, don't you? But you believe it because you need to.'

'You have no comprehension of the Russian mentality. They do not accept the sanctity of human life. They do not even grasp such a viewpoint. They have not even been told about things like that. They are so obedient. That is why so few can control so many.' He grunted, as if he was clearing his throat. 'I saw them in a village in East Prussia. They came in the early morning. The village was full of refugees, coming back from the front: Poles, Latvians, Estonians, Germans, women and children carrying what they could or pushing handcarts. It was autumn, and the rains had destroyed the roads, they were all covered in mud. The horses had all been taken away from them.

'The Russians came riding in on their tanks. They sent a spokesman into the village to tell the women and children that they had erected a mobile canteen on the other side of the hill. When all the women and children got there, we heard nothing but two machine guns. It went on and on. Some of those children were carrying little toys.'

Stenski stood up, moved towards the open door and went out. Johnson heard him close the front door behind him, and knew exactly where he was going: To have another look at the coffin.

$$\star \quad \star \quad \star$$

Snow fell the next day. It began in mid-morning, drifting down from a heavy laden sky and lay thick and moist. They waited in the house, Johnson peering out of the kitchen window into the white, ever changing curtain of snow.

The waiting: It was the one aspect which was never discussed and never recorded, and it reminded Johnson of his two years of National Service. There it could not be measured by the artificial activity of the parade ground or the pursuit of compulsory hobbies. Rather, it was the mindless hours hanging around for lorries to arrive, the desolate time on night exercise, in woodland or deserted farm outhouses, when nothing happened and nobody attacked and nobody retreated. It was the lost time, the useless time; the necessary evil of any organisation.

But Stenski could accommodate it. He spent the day sifting through papers which he kept in a folder. Johnson turned on the television when the programmes began in the early afternoon; and they sat together watching in the evening, as becalmed as two old ladies. The weather forecast at midnight was for more snow.

'Andrushenko comes tomorrow,' Stenski said when the programmes had finished. 'I have been thinking: Why do you not go over to the airport and have a look at him? You could do it from a discreet distance.' He went off and came back with the folder. There was a photograph in it, passport size. 'It was in the file in London, so I had a copy made. I expect his hair has thinned out, but the shape of the face will be the same.'

Johnson examined it with great care: A narrow face, not Russian at all. Dark hair had been brushed straight back from the forehead over the crown, in a style long disappeared. He had heavy, dominant eyebrows.

In the morning Stenski rang early for the car.

The journey lasted an hour, and the driver parked in a wide area behind the terminal building. He switched the engine off and said he would wait there. Johnson reflected that, for the driver, too, the waiting was an inescapable part of life. That was the sum of what they had in common.

In the main lounge, he consulted the arrivals and departures board. Flights were running normally, in spite of the snow. TU 220 was due in half an hour. He had a coffee and travelled, at his leisure, up an escalator to the observation roof. They were hiring binoculars at 20 schillings an hour and he took a pair. The wind was strong, plucking feverishly at his coat, and few had braved it just to look at aeroplanes. They were mostly children.

He scanned the horizon. Snow covered the fields but the runways were clear.

He heard the plane before he saw it, the

drone coming from far away. The children heard it, too, and gathered behind the clear plastic shield to watch. Then he did see it, a squat ungainly shape, fat as a pregnant pig, already low and its wheels down. It came on, losing height, until it seemed to brush its belly against the access road: But that was just the binoculars distorting the angles. At least, he hoped to God it was. It gained the runway itself, just beyond the banks of red lights at the end of the tarmac, and the wheels were feeling for concrete. The engines yearned as they were given reverse thrust but the impetus carried it a great way away. It returned slowly and stopped some distance away from all the other planes. A service jeep was towing a mobile metal stairway towards it. A bus appeared from below him and headed out to collect the passengers. Johnson trained the binoculars on the plane. A hammer and sickle had been painted on its tail fin and the word Aeroflot, in cyrillic alphabet, stretched above the row of port-hole windows. The passengers began to emerge from the opened door, the hostess — in pale blue uniform — smiling as they filed by. They came out quickly, as if they were anxious to be rid of the plane.

Johnson was sure he saw him. They wore fur hats and big coats, even the women, but the faces were not covered. Andrushenko came out near the end, one hand on the railing: A medium-sized man, not bulky even in all that clothing. He paused at the bottom of the stairway, turned his face away from the wind, and was gone into the bus.

The driver was reading a book when Johnson got back to the car. 'Somebody important must have come in,' the driver said, 'A dirty great black limousine was here to meet him. Probably a politician or a footballer.' He laughed to himself. It was a joke only chauffeurs would comprehend. 'Where do you want to go now? Back?'

Johnson muttered his assent. His hands and feet were damnably cold.

In one of the three villages off the main road, he made the driver stop while he found a grocery shop. He bought two litre bottles of milk, and some more of it in triangular cardboard cartons.

* * *

Johnson went to Vienna to collect the van next morning. Stenski had arranged everything by telephone. A pretty receptionist found the dossier while Johnson casually thumbed through the brochures on the counter. Twenty minutes later, they brought the van to the door. He had never driven one before and was glad they insisted on a test drive before they let him go on his own. He was surprised how bulky it was, and he drove slowly back to the house. Stenski was at the door. He must have seen the van coming. He walked forward and examined it with great care. 'It is certainly large enough for what we require,' he said.

'I'll reverse it into the garage,' Johnson said. 'There may be a frost tonight and we want the thing to start in the morning.'

Behind them, they could hear the persistent drip of water from the choked gutters as the snow melted a little.

'You are right. We must take no chances,' Stenski said. 'No chances at all.' He turned towards the house.

★   ★   ★

Snow had fallen in Berlin also. Barnard didn't care. It was the dampness which harrassed him and must, he swore, have gathered in his lungs like fungus in an old oil drum. He wore a heavy coat against it, almost a trench coat with a double row of leather buttons woven into the shape of knots, but that did no good. He still had to breathe the air.

He spent a day at the embassy, among the files. And he sent a request to McClellan, asking about Eva Karow. She didn't appear anywhere in the files. Did Stenski know about her? A messenger brought the reply, a single piece of telex paper in a brown envelope, next morning. The paper had a row of figures at the top — reference numbers, he supposed — and one curt sentence. Answer to query of 28/11 negative, repeat negative. So he rang Holmstangl. They were very helpful.

They had employed a blonde woman there, they said, but she had left three years ago. She was a secretary and her name was Eva Karow. She had known Atkins. The accounts department took a time to find her address and the man there did say that it was years old and she might have moved since. It was a street in Grunewald.

Barnard drove over.

The house was small and detached, with a garden running all around it. The occupant, a thin woman with two children — one held in the crook of her arm, the other tugging her skirt from behind — said Eva Karow had lived there but had moved. She had her new address somewhere, went back into the house and came back with it.

Auerbacherstrasse, near the railway station, number 27B. Not too far away. He left the car in the station car park and walked back. It was almost five in the evening and in the narrow street, the shops were closing. One, a pet shop, had a window full of wriggling puppies and kittens. A woman in an apron gathered them, from their wire pens. Barnard paused on the other side of the road. The blue street sign was fixed to the wall just above the pet shop: Number 27 was at the far end. He walked ponderously up the hill, the road flanked by houses with mature trees spreading branches out over the pavement. Darkness had come quickly. The street lamps were yellow, making the heaps of snow which had been cleared from the driveways into translucent shapes; they had begun to thaw and sunk back into cones of ice when the evening frost had arrested them. The snow on the pavement had been crushed and thinned by countless foot-marks. Now it crackled underfoot.

Number 27 was in a block of apartments towards the top of the hill. The block itself was 15 storeys of grey, precast concrete rising straight up into the night. Inside, Barnard examined the panel on the wall. Tenant's names were typed on cards and pushed into slots, A's to the left, B's to the right. He wanted floor twelve. He walked to the lift at the end of the corridor and pressed the oblong call button. It ascended slowly, made a whining noise as it arrived — as if it were exhaling breath — and the doors opened. The floor was pea-green, scuffed linoleum. The interior stank of human sweat. Somebody had pressed chewing gum onto the underside of the control panel and it had hardened, like the ice outside, into a cone. He stepped out at the twelfth, out onto a bare concrete landing. An empty coffee tin had been placed by the lift door for cigarette ends. He saw it dimly because there was only one light, a naked bulb hanging from unsecured flex which ran up and through a ragged hole in the plasterboard. The place wasn't finished.

He followed the corridor into the darkness, searching vainly for light switches and, at a junction, turned right. The doors were already numbered, but the apartments uninhabited. He struck a match and, peering forward, saw number 23. The flame consumed the match quickly, making its end curl as it reached down towards his fingers. He let it fall. The next door would be 25. He turned again into a narrow landing with an outside window to his left and a door to his right, a sliver of white light coming from under it.

They took him as he reached forward to knock.

The first blow cut him across the back of his neck and pitched him forward against the door; he thought his neck was broken. As he went down, a boot dug into his side, then a second. He half turned and saw, in the instant before the boot struck him again, two figures framed in the outline of the window frantic to get at him. He took another punch in the face as he came up and lunged at them, flailing his own fists; felt the boot in the pit of his stomach and fell again, his guts windless as a punctured tyre; half rose and sank back grasping something. A jacket. A lapel. A sleeve. He held it in his closed fist and dragged it down with him onto the concrete floor. The chilled surface grated his face, tearing the skin on one cheek. He was bleeding. He felt a face very close to his, the breath coming from it as tight and desperate as a hiss;

felt the man's body thrusting itself at him and he grabbed hair, moist with perspiration. He knew the second man was struggling to get at him, but he thought — suddenly, and with great clarity — that the fallen bodies must have blocked the corridor.

Barnard had the animal strength to tighten his fingers on the hair and hammer the head down onto the concrete once, twice, three times. Then the body was pushing over him, trying to batter him with both hands but weakly, as if the last impulses of instinct impelled him and nothing else.

Barnard heard the rustle of the man's clothing; felt the buckle of a trouser belt on his chest; then he forced the head down again. It made a short, sharp sound like a dry bone breaking. The man did not move again.

Barnard looked up and saw nothing but the second man leaning towards him, a blackened silhouette wielding a repulsive, inescapable power which was hypnotic and was going to destroy him. The blow was delivered from short range, two feet, perhaps less. It seemed to cleave his head from his shoulders. For a second, he had an unbearable pain directly behind his eyes. He was unconscious before he fell back onto the concrete for the last time.

He woke at dawn. He saw a crescent of dried blood arced up the wall; his own. Then the headache came, a pain which expanded and contracted like a pulse. His mouth was arid, and his tongue scoured it for moisture. At least his teeth weren't broken. His coat was torn at the shoulder, as if it had been clawed by an animal.

He tried to stand, but pain from his stomach prevented that. He inched towards the apartment door and pushed it with one hand. The door swung lazily back. The apartment was emply and unfurnished. Only a light bulb had been fitted. It was the light he had seen the night before, coming from under the door; it was still on.

He felt the darkness coming back, but he knew it was dawn — the absence of traffic noise told him that. The headache grew more insistent; the concrete floor in the corridor seemed to be paved with shadows. He drifted back into unconsciousness, thinking stupidly that his toes were already numb with the cold.

He had no memory of turning himself round and crawling to the lift, or calling out for help. He did remember the ambulance, its siren wailing, and, in it, a nurse bathing his face with a warm, moist flannel. He remembered voices in the ambulance, coming nearer, and discussing him in German he could not understand, then receding to the whispers of conspirators: a hospital trolley with wheels which creaked, being pushed with deliberate care; and the darkness again, swallowing the voices; a distant shuffling of feet near the bedside; the feel of female hands adjusting the pillow; and sleep.

⋆　⋆　⋆

He slept for two days. When the nurse told him that, he didn't believe it. He imagined that no amount of beating could do that to him. The room was small and square, with a washbasin on one wall and a towel on a rung beside it; and a white wardrobe, where his clothes would be. The window gave him a view of the lawns. All the snow had gone.

The Embassy sent an under-secretary to see him on the third day, a gaunt man in his early fifties with perfectly white hair. He sat, in diffidence, at the bedside when the nurse had brought him a wooden chair. His manner was almost that of a doctor.

'I do hope you are feeling better,' he said. 'Incidentally, this is a private room. We shall, of course, pay for it.'

'I'm very flattered,' Barnard said.

'Perhaps the irony of this has escaped you,' the man went on. He didn't like Barnard. 'I understand that this is the hospital they brought Atkins to. He was dead upon arrival, of course. Not like you.' He offered a bleak, watery smile.

Barnard said nothing.

'Do you know who was so brutal with you?'

'Not yet. I'll find out.'

'I thought you would say something

like that. I had rather hoped you would not. The doctors here are most emphatic: You will need a period of several weeks to convalesce. Your stomach has severe internal lacerations. They almost operated on you.' He was watching Barnard closely, appraising him. 'I have consulted London and they think you ought to be moved back to the United Kingdom as soon as you are well enough. That does seem a most reasonable view, if I may say so. In the meantime, they insist that you do as you are told and put yourself entirely in the hands of the doctors. They are very good here, you know.'

'Who did you talk to in London?' It was a challenge to the authenticity of what Barnard had just been told, and they both knew it.

'McClellan.'

'I didn't know you people had any contacts with security over there.'

'We do,' the man replied, revealing, just for an instant, a measure of conceit, 'when we need to.'

'I'll talk to them myself.'

'They imagined your response would

be something like that. Mr. McClellan gave me the most detailed instructions that on no account are you to be, permitted near a telephone. Forget all about Atkins and these other people. Of course McClellan understands that you would want to . . . to continue with your work. But he wants you to have a rest. He feels you have earned it, and I am sure he is correct.'

'I'm being taken off it?'

'I'm trying to tell you as gently as you will allow me. The case is closed. Mr. McClellan has decided that all investigations into the unfortunate death of Atkins will cease. He is convinced that no good can come of it. He did say you wouldn't take it very well. Such a civilised man. I had no idea he would be like that.'

Barnard yearned for a cigarette. 'You tell McClellan that I got beaten up for a reason — because I'm starting to get close, too damn close, maybe. They wanted to frighten me off. It half worked. They've frightened you off.'

'You really do not understand. How very difficult. Your little incident three evenings ago has been reported to the police. We are endeavouring to dissuade them from being too zealous, but they have already taken statements from the woman who found you in the flats and the doctor who went in the ambulance to collect you.

'They are anxious to take a statement from you. They wish to know why you were in the flats at all. Diplomatic immunity would not cover that. Furthermore, the secretary of the golf club where you went has complained officially about your conduct there. He wrote a very pungent letter indeed, and the ambassador takes a very serious view of matters like that.'

'I don't answer to him.'

'You appear to have an excellent — not to say intimate — understanding of violence, but little else. The ambassador has channels open to him which are denied to all others — he can ring the Foreign Secretary direct, if he needs to. Do you imagine that if he made such a telephone call, saying that you are a threat to all the goodwill we have fostered here over many years . . . do you imagine that you would not be recalled the same day? If it were necessary, the ambassador could order you to be physically placed on an aeroplane.'

'Do me a favour, since you seem to be a messenger,' Barnard said, needing to hurt him, 'and go back and tell the ambassador, and McClellan, that I came here to do a dirty job and I'm wading through the dirt now. What did they expect? A garden party? And tell them something else: If I go back to London, that's condoning the murder of Atkins. If your ambassador is so concerned, how does he feel about little Atkins getting his head broken in two? You tell him that it's about time the British stopped getting shoved around, terrified of letters from golf club secretaries.'

The man stood up, and buttoned his coat with crisp, neat movements. 'You are a fool. If I may descend to your kind of phraseology, you are a bloody fool.'

He moved towards the door. 'When the doctors decide that you are strong enough to travel, they will inform the Embassy.

You will be issued with an aeroplane ticket and you will go home that day. Frankly, I came here today to sympathise, but in your case it is difficult to summon. What do you want to do: Fight the whole world?' He reached the door and turned. 'However, I am sorry that you were so badly hurt.'

Barnard grunted something — he hadn't the grace or inclination to thank the man — and closed his eyes.

Fight the world, he thought. That's rich, that is. I tried it once — and only lost on points.

★  ★  ★

The under secretary came back a week later, but the receptionist told him that Mr. Barnard had discharged himself the previous evening. 'The night staff were on duty,' she said, 'so I do not know what happened. I have his dossier and treatment card here. It is marked: Closed.'

'He was not to be allowed to leave.'

'He could not have been prevented. There is no regulation which empowers us to keep a person in hospital against their wishes. Is that not the same in Britain?'

As he came out of the hospital, he reflected bitterly: Clever Mr. Barnard, clever enough to wait for the night shift, who probably didn't even know about the request from the Embassy.

He would inform McClellan that the bird had flown the nest, and counsel caution. He was very sure that clever Mr. Barnard would find himself back in hospital soon enough.

★   ★   ★

Barnard took a taxi to Grunewald, told the driver to stop at the end of the street, and paid him. He wondered about his car. The police would have picked that up by now. He walked slowly, but his stomach felt healed. He reached the little detached house and knocked just once. The woman came, anxiously peering round it. In the background, the baby was crying; the elder again stood behind her mother, the same nervous clinging to the skirt.

'Remember me?' Barnard said.

'No.'

'I came here ten days ago, asking about a woman who used to live here: Eva Karow.'

'Oh yes. Did you find her?'

'I found this.' He pointed to his cheek, the skin still raw.

'I am sorry,' she said, beginning to close the door. He pushed it crudely open, and went in. He hoped to God the neighbours weren't watching.

She feigned anger as he closed the door behind him. 'I just want to talk to you,' he said. He seemed bigger and squarer in the coat. 'I also got kicked in the stomach, and my favourite coat was badly damaged.' The shoulder had been sown at the hospital; but nothing could ever repair it properly.

She sent the girl off into the kitchen to look after her brother, who cried on. Barnard and the woman went into the lounge, sparsely furnished. He knew perfectly well that she was frightened.

'Who gave you that address?' he asked.

139

'I do not know what you are saying.' Her fingers were thinner than slender, and restless.

He looked straight at her. 'I came here looking for Eva Karow. You gave me an address. It was an apartment block, thirty minutes away from here. Just as I was about to knock on the door of number 27B, a very odd thing happened. Two men nearly beat me to death. They were waiting for me. It was very dark, and very convenient for them. They knew I was coming, and you are the only person who knew I was going there — and when.'

She was a spare woman who might have been pretty ten years before; but the child bearing had dried her up. The bones in her knees protruded.

'I do not understand,' she said.

'You understand. And don't get any silly ideas. I don't feel any inhibitions about the fact that you're a woman. With children.'

'Please go away now.'

'Who came here and gave you that address?'

'Nobody came here.'

'I'll show you my stomach, I'll show you the bruises they gave me.' The threat was pointed. 'Come here,' he called out and the little girl raced into the room, looking expectantly at her mother, a tiny, frail creature of perhaps six.

'It's all right,' the woman said. 'Go back now.'

The girl looked at Barnard with the instinctive distrust of a child, and went away.

The woman sat down. 'They told me you wouldn't return,' she said. 'They promised you wouldn't.' She was close to tears. 'I didn't want to do it, but they offered me money. I hate trouble, I can't protect the children from people like you. I can't even go to the police. What can they do? And then the people like you come back . . . '

'Who came?'

'Don't make me tell you.'

'You tell me.'

'Please.'

'You tell me.'

She began to cry, hands covering her eyes, softly, so that the children might not hear. 'Two men. I had never seen them before. They said somebody would probably come later and ask for the woman's address. All I had to do was direct you to the apartments. Eva Karow did live here, but she left nothing when she went.' She struggled to compose herself. 'I had to ring them when you had been.'

'What was the telephone number?'

'Please.' She opened her eyes, and looking up at him in mute supplication for pity, for understanding, for anything. 'If they did that to you, what will they do to me?'

'They won't come back here. Not after I've seen them.'

'They will. They told me that if I said anything to you, they would make trouble for the children.'

'What was the telephone number? Can you remember it?'

She shook her head.

'Yes you can.'

'It was a Grunewalde number with two sevens in it. 687739. I think it was that. I can't be sure.'

142

He was standing over her.

'I didn't even want their money. It's still in the drawer upstairs.'

'687739.' He said it slowly. 'Are you sure?'

She said yes. She was like the little girl; lost.

'Forget it ever happened.'

'Promise?'

'Promise.' It was a lie, but it was the best he could do.

'How did they know you would come here?'

'Somebody told them. Somebody at a golf club, I should think. Not that it matters.'

When he let himself out, the woman was sobbing again and her daughter was at her side, repeating helplessly: 'What's wrong, mummy?'

★   ★   ★

He went into a telephone booth in a cafe near the station and called the information service. It took the telephonist only a minute and a half to trace the address from the number.

It was lunch time. He lit another cigarette — I'm owed a few, he told himself, from ten days in bloody hospital — and went off to have a couple of beers. There was, after all, plenty of time.

★ ★ ★

The place was a house, designed like a bogus Bavarian chalet with false shutters at either side of the windows and a series of steps leading up to the front door. The walls had been sprayed with pebbledash, and painted white.

It was just after four. An upstairs light was on, bedroom or toilet, Barnard couldn't say. He didn't have a thing on him, no gun, no penknife, even, nothing which would pass as a weapon. He kept to the shadows, calculating that if he stood close to the front door when he knocked, he couldn't be clearly seen from any of the windows. They'd have to open the door to find out who it was. He climbed the steps. He rang the luminous bell three times. He'd done that before. It suggested a code which, even if the man inside did not recognise it, implied intimacy. He was already close to the door, and facing it so that his face was hidden. He heard curtains being drawn back high above, footsteps, and a light came on downstairs. The door was unbolted. He kicked it as hard as he could and thrust himself in. The man was half wedged behind it when Barnard seized him. It was all instinct: A knee between the legs, the rabbit punch to the neck, the knee full into the face as the body buckled downward. The man fell away onto the lounge carpet, and Barnard closed the door.

The man had a bandage wrapped round his head, low, like a visor, over the left eye.

'Where's your friend?' Barnard asked.

'Out.'

'I thought so. Only one light on.' He came into the room. 'We've met before.' The man was short and dressed in jeans and sweater. He lay on his back. 'How's your poor old head?' Barnard took him by the hair and lifted him to his feet, then

145

kicked his ankle. The man went down again with a cry and rolled onto his side, both hands clutching the ankle. 'It's broken.' Barnard surveyed the room: Old revolutionary posters on the walls, a record player on the floor, and piles of records strewn around it. No television. A place for elderly students. 'I do hope your friend doesn't come back,' Barnard said slowly. 'I wouldn't like that.'

The man was breathing hard, holding all the pain in. His hands had tightened round the ankle in a tourniquet.

'I'll give you a choice,' Barnard said. 'You can have it any of three ways. Young things like you — I bet you like coffee and I bet you've a kettle. I'm going to boil it and then pour the water over your head, your ankle or your balls. Which do you want?'

The man swore.

'Stay there,' Barnard said. 'That's my little joke. You couldn't even crawl, never mind run way.' He found the kettle on a shelf in the kitchen, filled it and switched it on; came back to the lounge. 'When is your friend due back?'

'You mean Klaus?'

'If that's his name.'

'I don't know. He went away after lunch in the car.'

The kettle began to hiss. There was a click as it turned itself off.

'Choose.'

'What do you want?'

Barnard had anticipated more resistance. 'Just some questions. Who do you work for?'

'Nobody. I'm unemployed.'

'Let you and I understand each other. My interest in you extends to the information you are going to give me. Otherwise, I'll use the kettle.'

'They'll kill me.'

'That's your problem.'

The man turned away from Barnard. 'I can't take this pain much longer,' he said.

'I'll ring the hospital when we've finished. The faster the better for you.'

'How did you find this house?'

'Never mind. Who do you work for?'

'We're hired. I don't even know the names. Klaus deals with that side of it. He handles the administration.'

'Who hires you?'

'They'll kill me.'

'I'll break the other ankle. Try me. I'll break it so it hangs loose. You'll never walk again without a stick.'

'A woman.'

'Name?'

'Name! I don't know. Klaus does.'

Barnard bent down. Their faces were very close. 'Give me the name.'

'Eva Karow.'

'Ever heard of a man called Atkins?'

'No.'

Barnard gripped his hair again.

'For God's sake,' the man said.

'Atkins?' Barnard almost spat the name.

'No.'

'All right, all right. Klaus knows all the names. Atkins, a little Englishman walking a dog. Killed a month ago in the Volkspark in Mariendorf. Beaten to death.'

'We don't kill people. Klaus didn't kill you. You get thirty years for that in this country.' He fell back onto the carpet. 'We only lean on people.'

'Did Klaus kill Atkins, all by himself?'

He shook his head. 'I've known him for fifteen years. We were at school together. We have never done anything like that.' The sweat from under his armpits had seeped out in patches onto the sweater. 'Call the hospital. Tell them to send an ambulance.'

'How do I find the woman?'

'She always rings us.'

'So you go out and beat people up because some woman just rings you up and asks you to?'

'She sends money in advance. The phone is over there. Ring for an ambulance.' The leg was doubled under his body as if, by pressing down on the ankle, he might relieve a measure of the pain.

'Who have you leant on before?'

'Klaus knows the names.'

'Jungermann? Manstein?'

The man shook his head. 'Who cares about names?'

'So there's only one question left. Just this one, and then I'll ring. How do I find Eva Karow?'

'I've told you. I don't know.'

'Last chance.'

'Klaus knows. I don't. He doesn't talk to me about those things.'

'Have it your way. I'm going now. Ring the hospital yourself.'

'I can't move. Look at me. You did that.'

Barnard shrugged.

'All right,' the man said. 'She lives in the east. You have to leave messages with an old woman. Listen, ring the hospital.'

'Telephone number in the east?'

'Schlidow 29 27 03. The old woman is stupid. You have to spell it all out for her. She doesn't hear very well. Say you want to leave a message for Eva. Just Eva. No surname. You have to go to the east, she doesn't come here. There is a cafe on the Unter Den Linden called the Happy Labourer. You sit by the door and wait for her.'

'If there happens to be a reception committee waiting when I get over there — if by any chance either you or Klaus happen to have warned them — within 30 minutes you will face a charge of murdering Atkins and assaulting me. You will be put away for a long time. Unless I get to you first.'

Stenski stood at the window, looking alternately at his wristwatch and the sweep of the valley. Johnson had already changed into a dark blue suit, and was sitting at the kitchen table nursing a cup of coffee.

'Don't go near him too soon,' Stenski said. 'Wait until they've had a lot to drink. The women have been taken care of. Incidentally, they are being paid a great deal of money. They are all professionals. The aftermath should be straightforward.' He scanned the drifting snow which lay in neat contours across the furrows of the ploughed field beyond the lawn. 'The invitation was the most delicate part. I mean the invitation to Andrushenko. It had to be very unofficial. The Embassy here are most impressive. Quite unlike Berlin. They have the most amazing contacts.' He glanced at his watch again.

'This is my last one. Either way. But we'll win, you and I, we'll win the last one. What will you do then?'

'I'll go back and discuss it with London. Maybe it's my last one, too.'

'But you are so young — you have so much to give them.' He was searching for the headlights in the distance, not finding them. 'I told that driver to be prompt. I stressed it. I stressed it as strongly as I could. That driver — such an ignorant man. Obtuse and ignorant. I wonder how they ever came to employ him? Do you notice it in his attitude? I am told he has been here for years and speaks no German.'

'Relax,' Johnson said. 'It's only half past six. I don't have to be there until eight.'

'That is not the point. The driver was instructed to be here at half past six.' Stenski was moving towards the anger of unreason, as he often did over petty matters. 'All this planning could be destroyed by a fool like him.' His eyes moved ceaselessly across the acres of ill-defined snow. 'I will have him dismissed. Perhaps he will understand that,

152

however ignorant he is. He has probably stopped somewhere for a few drinks. I know the kind. Careless, thoughtless . . . '

'Have a cup of coffee.'

'No! How can you consume so much of it? Most unhealthy.'

At that moment, deep in the valley, Stenski saw the headlights. 'That had better be him,' he said. He watched them come, threading a way towards the house. When the car had pulled up and the driver had entered the house Stenski said furiously: 'Look at the time.' He brandished his watch as if it were damning evidence.

'They told me seven o'clock,' the driver replied. 'It's only twenty to seven. They said it was important so I made sure I was early.'

Stenski, mute and impotent, left the room.

'Coffee?' Johnson asked as civilly as he could.

* * *

Johnson found Stenski in the lounge, at the window again. 'I'm going now. The

153

roads are bad so I'll take my time.'

'Better to be prudent,' Stenski said. 'Better by far.' His hands were interlocked behind his back: The favourite posture. 'Bring him back,' he whispered. 'Bring him back to me.'

Johnson did drive slowly. Through the three villages, he turned left onto the Vienna road. Gravel had been spread, and the fragments grated noisily against the underbelly of the car. He turned left again at the next crossroads and began to climb towards more hills.

He was more than nervous now.

He saw the hand-painted wooden sign nailed to a post at the roadside which said: The Phoenix, next right. He saw the mansion, briefly, through the conifer trees at the end of the garden, and was driving up a looping driveway which ended in a circle before the house, with another conifer tree in the grass-covered island in the middle of it; parked the car behind others ranged along the rim of the drive, and walked towards the house. A maid directed him to the barn at the rear. He heard the music before he reached it. The barn, a long, low building, had fairy lights strapped under the eaves of the tiled roof. The walls were old planks held against heavy timbers by wooden pegs. The entrance was at the far end, a doorway edged in more timber, off-true, as if it had been frozen at the moment of collapse.

The American was waiting just inside. A young woman stood at his side wearing a gown covered in sequins. The position was strategically perfect for welcoming guests.

'Good evening,' Johnson said. 'I'm Alan. Alan Douglas.'

'It's just great you could make it, Alan,' the American said. He had no idea who any Mr. Alan Douglas was supposed to be. Maybe, thought Johnson, he invites anybody and everybody. They shook hands solemnly. The woman went away with his coat. The American was a tall man with a big stomach. He wore a check suit and brown shoes, not quite the thing for an evening party — even if he was throwing it. Money but no style, an unhappy combination.

'Go on in and make yourself right at

home. Glad you could meet with us tonight.'

Johnson passed into the main room, a converted and restored baronial hall. At the far end, a log fire burned and a few guests had gathered within range of its warmth. Along the left hand wall, three teenage girls stood poised behind a long trestle table heavy with food. White cardboard plates were heaped at points along it, awaiting the onslaught. Two waiters in white tunics moved unobtrusively among the guests, bearing silver trays of assorted drinks, mostly gins and small bottles of tonic.

The American had followed him. 'We like to have parties now and again,' he said. He wasn't boasting, and he wasn't excusing the indulgence. It was all natural. But the party: That was designed to impress the American community. That was why so many different people had been invited. My God, Johnson thought, the Russians will be a real capture for him. Real live Russians — enough to give the fattened, middle-aged American women present more than goose-pimples.

156

As he was steered towards a group of seven or eight people, Johnson began to look for Andrushenko. He probably hadn't arrived yet. It was only twenty past eight.

The pop group, three men with long hair and jeans, nearly a uniform for their sort, had been resting on their stand in a corner of the room. They began to play again. One at the back moved frantically between an array of drums. The other two stood in front of him, plucking guitars.

Johnson dutifully shook hands with a few people and positioned himself at the rear of a group, facing the door.

He looked at his watch. Nine o'clock. There were 50 guests now, milling round like cattle in a field. Come on, Andrushenko, where are you?

He was edgy. The whole thing was a risk, even Stenski hadn't tried to deny that. And still Andrushenko didn't come.

The host returned, drew him to one side and whispered confidentially: 'We'll liven it up a bit later on. When the pensioners have been safely tucked in bed.' He winked, heavily and obviously.

'I've one or two surprises lined up.'

Johnson saw movement at the door. Two men. He was standing twenty feet away and could see them clearly. One short, one tall. He felt a current of excitement and, at the same moment, a short stabbing pain at the base of his spine, as he always did when he was excited.

Andrushenko was the shorter, a neat little man in a grey suit and blue tie with sallow skin and big eyes. His dark hair was swept straight back from his forehead. Johnson almost laughed. He hadn't changed his style from the photograph, and that was twenty years. He surveyed the room by instinct, morose and distrustful. The companion was obviously his driver. He wore a casual jacket and flannel trousers. Andrushenko had moved to one wall and stood engrossed in conversation with his companion.

At some unseen signal, people began to drift over to the food tables and eat. Johnson watched the Russians carefully. They kept their distance from everybody else, but took a whisky from a waiter. No water, he noticed. While the waiter stood, Andrushenko poured a whisky into himself and took another. The tall one did most of the listening, Andrushenko most of the talking.

The eating lasted half an hour. When it was over, the older people began to leave. It was almost ten now, the timing perfect. Then the girls came in.

The American had positioned himself in the middle of the floor. 'Ladies and gentlemen,' he said in a loud voice, 'I hope you're having a good time. When I got down to organising this party, I thought it wouldn't be such a bad idea to invite a few people who work goddam hard and, what's more, do the work that has to be done. I'm talking about the nurses. So I took myself along to a hospital in the big city and invited a bunch of them over. I'm so happy they could make it.' With a sweep of his hand, he indicated the ten girls standing, looking like orphans, just inside the door. Everyone applauded politely. 'Hey,' he said smiling broadly, 'come on in, the party's all yours.' The girls melted into the centre of the room. Two gravitated towards the Russians, and soon all four were talking.

At exactly ten thirty, the pop group stopped playing and the lights went down.

The American made his speech. 'My good friends — and particularly to good old Uncle Sam who, by the way, is paying for all this, although he doesn't know it — we have a session of letting our hair down over here in Austria once in a while. Now the other day, I was in Munich on business and during my visit they told me to go to a certain night club to see a certain act because, they said, it's just a sensation. I couldn't afford the time. You know how hard I work.' The laughter rose round him, dutiful and short-lived. 'They did warn me that I'd need to be pretty broadminded. Well, friends, I am broad-minded.' Only the native English speakers caught the nuance. 'I was curious, I'll admit to that. I do like art.' The same obedient laughter. 'So I got to thinking to myself: George, you're having a bit of a party next week in Vienna so why not hire them yourself, and then see if they are a sensation? So trade was done. You know me, friends. If old George wants something, old George generally ends up getting it. All right,' he said. 'Damned if I'm going to stand up here and make a fool of myself any longer. Let's get this show on the road. Ladies and gentlemen, here they are: The Stengels'.

They seemed to come from nowhere, just as the lights were totally extinguished and there was a whispering silence among so many people watching. The man and the woman stood absolutely still before the fire, and the aura of its glow invested them with a beautiful purity and dignity. Music began, civilised music. They wore skin-tight, flesh coloured garments, and the woman had long, blonde hair which tumbled down over her slender shoulders in a cascade. The man was fractionally taller, broad at the shoulder, with the strong legs of a trained athlete.

As the music reached a pitch, they moved together, embraced, separated and, while the man remained motionless, the woman weaved in a circle around him as if she was being drawn ever closer to him. She stood before him, running her hands up and down his chest.

She sighed and let her head fall onto his shoulder. His hands moved insistently over her breasts.

She bent her whole body forward and moved away from him in one fluid movement, then turned to face him. The game was to tease . . .

Johnson looked round. Andrushenko was watching intently, a full glass of whisky in his hand. This should get him in the mood, the ritual of public sex, the malt in the scotch . . .

Unconsciously, the dancer lifted the hair which had fallen across her face and brushed it away with a hand, went to her partner and began pressing against him, rotating her hips to the music. He closed his eyes. But when his hands went behind her to hold her still, and draw her small pelvis into him so he could push hard at her, she slipped away again, and waited, like his prey, a few feet away. The music was becoming louder, deeper, faster. He caught her hand as he advanced, used it as a lever to turn her round and, her back pressed against his chest, dug his finger tips into her belly, but harder now, and more urgently.

She made a noise drawn between a sigh and a moan. And his hands slipped down between her legs, openly foraging. She seemed to be struggling, half protest, half pleasure. But he crooked one of his arms around her neck and locked it so that she was helpless while the other played on her thighs, rising, as suddenly and swiftly as the tongue of a snake, back to the softness of the haven between her legs.

His hand went inside her costume at the waist and moved down. She opened her legs very wide, granted him an instant of freedom there; and broke away from him.

The music had stopped. A log on the fire, charred at its base, fell forward into the greying rim of ashes on the hearth.

The dancers drifted together, halted at arms length, looked into each other's eyes, and undressed.

Johnson turned away from them. Andrushenko was watching like a man hypnotised.

The garments were cast away into the shadows at the side of the fire and music, almost tribal in pitch and intonation, began again. They embraced, and the man lowered the woman onto the floor. She lay on her back across the front of the fire so that the yellow, molten pattern of flames seemed to play on her body, licking it. The man stood between her opened legs, tall and serene. With an imperious gesture, she threw her head back and the honeyed hair spread out around it in a pool. He knelt, at the altar which she had created for him. It might have been an illusion — professional, rehearsed, and fully prepared — but they seemed hungry to make love.

They finished just as the music did. The timing was perfect, right to the end. When the lights came on again, the dancers had gone.

'Let's dance, everybody,' the American shouted, exultant.

The lights were dimmed again. The

Russians were still talking to the girls, but Johnson understood the power of what they had all just seen: Public sex, well performed, was one of the most depraving stimulants, bordering almost on perversion. And Andrushenko must have been thinking: The girls are ripe for it. That would be nice for his ego, too.

A petite girl walked up to Johnson. 'Hello,' she said in English. 'I'm Tania.' Johnson smiled, not committing himself either way. 'Won't you ask me to dance?' He nodded. They danced classically, he holding her at a discreet distance. 'Everything is going well,' she said. 'But nobody said we were supposed to be nurses. That makes it complicated.' When the music ended, she led him over to the Russians. 'I'm sorry,' Tania said to them, 'but I don't know your names.' The Russians shook hands with Johnson, but did not give their names. She introduced him to the girls: 'Elizabeth and Renate.'

Johnson felt very hot, the kind of heat which wells up inside and threatens to choke.

'They are Bulgarian businessmen,'

Renate said, indicating the Russians. Andrushenko was obviously suspicious. Perhaps that was his nature. His eyes, in fact, were greygreen, and seemed to peer out of darkened caves beneath his eyebrows. They moved ceaselessly. He smelt of hair lotion. The other said nothing, and Johnson was sure he was just a driver. Both had drunk a good deal already.

'Don't you dance?' Johnson asked Andrushenko in German.

Andrushenko shrugged, held up the glass in his right hand, half full of whisky, and parted his lips in a faint smile, indicating that a man must get his priorities right. But Renate, looking almost coy, grasped his sleeve. He raised the glass to his mouth and emptied it, walked swiftly to one of the tables where he deposited the glass, came back and took Renate away into the swaying mass of couples. The other followed exactly, even placing his empty glass next to that of Andrushenko.

Johnson guided Tania up to the other end of the room and when they were dancing, a little closer now, whispered — as intimately as if it had been words of love — 'don't push them too hard, let them make the running.'

'There will be no difficulties,' she said. 'I know what those two men want.'

'So do I. And they'll want to do it in the girl's flat. They've nowhere of their own. They both live inside . . . inside the embassy. Not possible there.'

'Not possible in a nurses' home, either. We are supposed to be nurses.'

At midnight, twenty couples remained.

Only then did Johnson and Tania rejoin the Russians. They were drunken now, and the girls were leading them gently on. Renate's blouse was half open, but she didn't seem to care.

Tania said it. 'The party will be over soon. Why don't we all go on somewhere else?'

The girls agreed. Andrushenko's eyes were moving again, but dulled by the drink.

'My place is not too far away,' Johnson said. 'I've got some drink up there, enough anyway. Let's invite a few more people, keep the party spirit going.' That's what he must do: reassure the Russians. Everything must be natural.

Tania said: 'Perhaps it is not such a good idea to invite other people. I thought we might all want to make it a more intimate occasion.'

'All right,' Johnson said. 'It's all the same to me.'

He took care not to meet Andrushenko's eyes with his own.

Andrushenko turned to his companion and spoke in Russian, then nodded. From that moment, which had been ordinary and innocent — and which Johnson had dreaded for a week — all the possibilities were opened up. He could picture the gaunt figure of Stenski, waiting at the window, ignoring the driver . . . and, barely twenty yards away, the garage with the heap of leaves in the corner . . . and the coffin . . .

'Have you a car?' Johnson asked.

Andrushenko nodded again. You could always tell which of two men was dominant: The one people naturally directed questions at.

'When we have collected our coats, just follow me.'

The American was by the door. By now, he had forgotten everybody's name and just stood, affable and ineffectual, shaking hands with departing guests.

Outside, the Russians and the two girls got into a black Opel which had been parked down the driveway near the road. Andrushenko sat in the back with Renate, a slim girl in her early twenties with short, curly hair. A better class of tart, Johnson had mused, when he had first seen her. Elizabeth was in the front with the other Russian. She was taller, and fuller, than Renate. She had a sad, failed air about her and pallid skin.

Johnson took the Mercedes very slowly, keeping the Opel in vision in the rear mirror. Tania sat back in the seat and wanted to make polite conversation.

'They are strange men. Prehistoric. Most wouldn't have needed all that prompting, and a formal discussion — they would have jumped right in.' She wore a trouser suit in blue and white; she had crossed her legs and lit a cigarette.

'Are they really Bulgarians?'

'Of course they are. What did you think?'

'Sorry I asked.'

They reached the main road and Johnson waited until the Opel had caught them up before he turned on to it. The Opel followed forty yards away and he could see the driver, stiff and mechanical, handling the car very correctly. That's what Johnson would have expected: Caution. They'd be told a hundred times to be careful, not to get involved in traffic offences.

'You look nervous,' Tania said. 'Just watch the road, will you, and relax.'

His elation had gone and the brooding returned. He would have wished, if he had been other than what he was, to stop the car and abandon it; tell this woman to get lost, and just walk away, lose himself in the pine trees up the hillside, and never come back. He glanced in the mirror. The headlamps were still there, constant in the darkness, like a harness attached to him. It was all crazy. How had Stenski sold it to London?

The house was held in darkness. He parked near the front door and waited until the Opel came to a halt behind. The fresh snow was soft under his feet as he got out and motioned for the others to follow. 'Come on in,' he called. Renate opened the rear door of the Opel, her coat flapping, struggling awkwardly to do up the buttons on her blouse. It was open all the way down to the waist. Andrushenko walked at her side as if to emphasise, by his proximity, that she was his property. The other locked the car meticulously, checking all four door handles. Elizabeth was already inside the house when he had finished. Johnson switched the electric fire on in the lounge, and assured them the room would warm up in a minute.

'Drink?' he asked. They all began to sit down. 'Scotch, Scotch — and for you, my dear, another Scotch? That makes three. Gin for you, Elizabeth? Tania: Scotch, too. Coffee as well? Six Coffees.' He poured the drinks first. He'd bought the bottles a couple of days before: A whisky, a gin, a brandy, some soda. That was all.

The three bottles looked meagre and obvious on a side table. He'd had to buy glasses as well. Alone in the kitchen, he found the cups and remembered there were no saucers. They wouldn't mind that. He was a business man abroad, and he couldn't be expected to have everything.

The tablets were in a thin, plastic tube in the cupboard with sliding doors. The doors went back easily, and he brought the tube down. The tablets were perfectly white. He held the tube at an angle, and allowed two tablets to fall into the palm of his left hand.

He had placed two cups apart from the others on the tray and, into these, he put one tablet each. They dissolved at the touch of the boiling water, fizzing briefly. He stirred both cups laboriously.

There is a moment in an operation, he was thinking, when it acquires a force of its own, just like an aeroplane. A lot of people are involved, and as it takes off, it's too late to switch the engines off. They were already past the critical point. Nobody could call it off any more, too many were already enmeshed . . . the Russians, the women, Stenski . . . Johnson wished to God he'd had the guts to stop the Mercedes and go away into the trees.

When he took the tray into the lounge, Andrushenko already had Renate's blouse open again and she was trying to keep him at bay. He was no longer aware of people around him.

'Hey,' Johnson said in German in a good natured kind of way, 'this is a party, not an orgy: Plenty of time for that later.' Andrushenko looked sheepish, and Renate became very prim. She did the buttons up quickly. 'Have a cup of coffee.' The yellow cup. Johnson placed the tray on the table next to the three bottles and handed the cups out individually. No mistakes now. Where was Stenski? In the garage, probably, near the coffin. They all drank. Andrushenko wrapped his hand right round the coffee cup, ignoring the handle. But he only sipped at it. The stuff must have been too hot after all the whisky.

Johnson sat in a chair, and Tania lowered herself onto his lap. The press of warm flesh pleased him. Andrushenko was on the other chair, Renate on his lap, too. The other Russian sat on the sofa, Elizabeth keeping her distance. He seemed unsure of how much he was permitted. From moment to moment, he sought Andrushenko's eyes for a sign.

They talked for a few minutes, precisely until the coffee was finished. Andrushenko was given more whisky and began on Renate again. She said: 'I don't like too much in public.' He grunted something. Johnson stood up. 'Let's all go upstairs,' he said. Renate went to the door and Andrushenko followed, meek as a child. 'Back bedroom,' Johnson called up the stairs after them, 'I want the front one.' They all laughed.

The other Russian remained on the sofa, a frozen, unbending profile of a man. Still he had not ventured near Elizabeth and now, the chance to be granted permission had gone. 'Have fun,' Johnson said to him, but he was unsure how much German he understood.

He and Tania went to the front bedroom. Tania immediately sat on the bed. Muffled sounds came through the dividing wall. 'I hope you don't get any ideas,' she said. 'I'm not part of the package.'

He sat next to her. 'I wish you were.'

'Forget it. I'm a very happily married woman. I don't ever entertain clients myself.' She was hard now, and the transition to hostility had been made effortlessly.

The sounds suggested a struggle from the other bedroom. Renate moaned — pain, not pleasure. 'Christ, he's going to kill her,' Johnson said. He looked at Tania for some sort of guidance.

'She's a very capable girl. A little violence is an occupational hazard. Some people like that.'

'You don't know him.'

They sat until the next moan. They went into the back bedroom together. Renate was on her knees on the bed, her hands closely bound behind her back by Andrushenko's tie, his handkerchief stuffed into her mouth. He was arched over her back. He hadn't even bothered to take his shirt off.

He looked absurdly like an old bull.

His eyes were closed. He slipped off the girl and fell gently onto the bed beside her, on his back. His legs were narrow and white, with veins as big as welts threaded up them.

At least the tablet had worked. Johnson untied the girl. She wrung her wrists. 'Nobody told me that kind of thing was going to happen,' she said. She was very angry. 'He nearly tore me to pieces. He went mad. I called out. Didn't you hear me?' She turned on Tania, accusing. 'He had his hand over my mouth.'

'Get dressed,' Johnson said.

'I wasn't warned.'

'Shut up,' Johnson said. 'You're not exactly the virgin queen. And you're getting well paid.'

She took her clothes into a corner of the room and dressed with her back to them.

Downstairs, the other Russian had gone quietly. He had slipped to one side of the sofa and lay, motionless and angular. The girl, quite untouched, observed him with curiosity. These things happen.

Johnson loaded the three women out into the Mercedes. As he switched it on, he turned towards the garage. There, behind the window and peering through the ivy, he saw Stenski's face. Stenski made no sign, sought nothing from Johnson, no gesture to confirm success, no warning of failure.

It was almost four in the morning when Johnson got back from dropping them in Vienna.

★ ★ ★

Stenski was in the kitchen. 'I have administered both the injections,' he said. 'I have never done that before. It would have been better done by a qualified doctor. Their flesh is spongy, like dough; not as warm as I had anticipated.'

'One of the girls was very upset.'

'Andrushenko's girl?' Stenski asked.

'Yes.'

'I warned about his tastes. I am not surprised. He appears to be the very worst kind of Russian, Asiatic rather than European,' Stenski consoled himself. 'But he will be useful. More than that. Priceless. Quite priceless.'

'How long does the injection last for?'

'Long enough. The Embassy doctor offered me no guarantees. Just like a doctor. They cultivate their mystery. Not that it matters. The other one in the lounge will just lie there until we have gone.'

'What do we do now?'

'Try and rest. We must be up at five thirty. The flight is at ten forty.'

Johnson went into the lounge and surveyed the Russian. He had slipped further down and now lay on his side along the length of the sofa. Johnson selected one of the armchairs, arranged the cushion behind his head and tried to cat-nap. He opened his eyes only once, but, even in the darkness, could see the outline of the Russian. He imagined the Russian moved. You're nervous, he told himself. The Russian's breathing was gentle but curiously uneven, as if he was not inhaling, only exhaling.

Stenski was in the kitchen, of course. Johnson could see the light on. He would be there, sitting at the table with all the documents laid out before him, checking them again. He was as careless about sleep as he was about food: he dispensed with either or both when it suited him. 'They do say,' he had once observed in Berlin, 'that depravation sharpens the intellect. It could be true.'

★   ★   ★

It was a godless, greying dawn shared only by the forsaken people who were ending a night of work, or those going early to it. The lounge was cold and desolate. The sour smell of tobacco lingered. Stenski had woken him, tugging, just once, at his sleeve. Johnson felt abominably stiff after a night in the chair. He looked at his watch. Five fifteen. He had slept only an hour. His eyes were hot and tired; the taste of whisky remained in his mouth, as soured as the tobacco smell. He felt dishevelled, as he always did when he slept with his clothes on. The rims of his shirt sleeves were soiled at the wrists, and he knew that the loosened collar would be, too.

The Russian had not moved.

It was the half-light. He made himself a cup of coffee and took it upstairs while he shaved. Stenski had become agitated at the prospect of Johnson spending time shaving, but Johnson had been insistent. 'I'm supposed to be in mourning. I can't look like a tramp,' he said.

'Well hurry.'

Andrushenko still lay on the bed, his trousers bunched round his ankles. There seemed a pure justice in that: A dirty old man held in the very posture which exposed precisely what he was.

Johnson put on a white shirt, then the black tie and suit. He had black gloves which Stenski had produced from somewhere, but they were a size too small and he planned to carry them to complete the image. When he went back downstairs, Stenski was at the kitchen table. He wanted to check the documents again.

'For Christ's sake,' Johnson said. 'It's too late now. It's too late to stop. If the papers are not authentic, that's too bad.'

'One mistake,' Stenski might almost

have been waving a finger in admonition. 'Study all the great murder cases, and you will discover how intrepid the thinking criminal can be.' He had his coat on, his hat on the table, ready. 'It is always the most trivial matters which are their undoing: The tie-pin, the tooth-brush, the wrong shoe-polish. I have tried to eliminate that. Some people work in a different way. They rush about leaving a trail of havoc. I should not be surprised at all if that is what Mr. Barnard is doing at this moment in Berlin.'

'You really didn't like him, did you?'

'Physically he was a man. In the important matters, an adolescent.'

'But you've got to have people like that.'

'The Germans used to think so. I'm sorry. It's not a good comparison.'

They dressed Andrushenko together. There would have been a degree of farce in that, if the circumstances had been different, because a man who is inert is very difficult to manoeuvre; the limbs are loose and do not respond to manipulation. When they had finished, they left him on the bed and went to the garage. Stenski was wearing the hat and looked like an undertaker. Daylight was seeping across the sky, spreading pastel shades of blue and cream and white. They could see right down the valley, almost as far as the main road. The coffin was heavier than Johnson had expected. They had to try three times before they forced their fingers under it, brushing the chill concrete. They lifted it and carried it towards the opened rear doors of the van. They laid the lid alongside it, and Johnson backed the van up to the front door of the house.

In the end, only Johnson's strength made everything possible. He knew how heavy a human body is — he had seen, in London years before, a woman faint at the counter of a pub, and two men vainly try to shift her dead weight.

Now, aided by Stenski, he hauled and levered Andrushenko onto his back and humped him, without ceremony, down to the van. They almost had to drag him into the interior, and getting him into the coffin itself was more difficult still because the space they had was cramped and they had to squat, knees bent. Eventually they lifted him and almost dropped him in. They pressed the lid down and Johnson put the screws in. 'I hope the breathing holes are big enough,' he said.

'They will be. I had them checked by the doctor who gave me the tablets and the injections. He passed them as adequate. Incidentally, the holes are on all the sides so it doesn't matter which way they lay it in the aeroplane, or what they stack against it — even if we are not given the special compartment they normally use for coffins. And we have been promised that.'

'What happens when they find the mark the needle made on the other Russian?'

'They won't. It makes only a slight impression. Normally, unless he has some skin disorder, it heals completely within ten hours.' Stenski seemed partially content. Johnson wanted only to wash his hands after touching Andrushenko.

Stenski would countenance nothing like that. 'We must leave immediately,' he said. 'We don't want too many people to see the van. Fortunately the Austrians are not like the Germans. Most of them will still be asleep.'

As they moved off, Stenski said: 'The other Russian is in a difficult position. He spent a night out, after drinking a lot. He was involved with a woman, although he will certainly claim that he did not touch her. We cannot know whether they will believe that. Andrushenko is gone. However the other man tries to explain that, he will be in a situation one would not envy. In any case, they will spend a week at least checking the details. They are very slow-witted.'

'What if they find the woman Maria?'

'She can tell them nothing, nothing at all. She doesn't know anything. Unless you talked . . . '

'Don't be silly.'

When they reached the airport, Johnson parked the van outside a building marked: Air Freight. Stenski remained while he entered through a swing door.

There were three counters: Inland, Ausland, Claims. None was manned. The floor smelt of polish. A stack of suitcases and packages lay against one wall. At the Ausland counter, he had to call out for service. A small man, looking like a railway porter, came from a door at the back smoking a cigarette.

'I've brought some freight,' Johnson said and realised, too late, that the word was quite wrong. 'It is booked on the Copenhagen flight this morning. The 10.40.'

'What was the name?'

'Henderson. English.'

That was wrong, too. Stenski had been emphatic: Don't volunteer anything. Just answer the questions.

The man produced a ledger and ran his finger down the list of names. 'Not here,' he said with finality. The cigarette was still in his mouth, but had gone out. 'When was it booked in?'

'A few days ago.'

He turned the pages of the ledger, going backwards. 'What exactly is it?'

'A coffin. My wife died nine days ago,

185

and I'm taking her home to Sweden.'

'Oh, that.' The man was looking carefully at him. 'You should have said so in the first place. They're kept in a different book. This one is for personal things. You would be surprised what people want to send. Here it is . . . Henderson. Your wife was called Helga?'

Johnson nodded.

'Where is the coffin now?'

'In a van outside.'

'Well, the thing is, we'll carry it as far as the customs, then you have to go through the customs with it yourself. You show them all the revelant documents. We can't do that. Once the documents have been checked and the coffin cleared, we take it out on to the plane. You just come back and wait in the passengers' lounge like any normal passenger.'

Johnson nodded again. He was beginning to feel uncomfortable.

'Where did you say the van was?'

'Outside the door.'

'Take it round to the shed marked Three. They'll do the rest.'

Stenski had sunk into one of his distant

moods when Johnson returned.

'No problems,' Johnson said. 'Shed Three. I will have to accompany it into the customs. This is the big one — a risk, and I don't care what you think.'

'Customs officers are generally stupid,' Stenski observed. 'That is why they do the work they do, and not something more demanding.' Certain situations, or certain types of people, produced in him this strange, unfeeling contempt. He regarded minor officials everywhere as an irritation; he could be incredibly surly with them when he chose.

Shed Three was an old aircraft hangar. Now it was packed with freight, mostly in wooden crates bound by wire, with names and numbers branded onto them. A foreman was directing a fork-lift. Johnson went to him.

'Coffin?'

'My wife.'

'I'm sorry.'

Behind him, the truck had begun to move some crates marked 'Produce of Malawi'.

'Four men for a coffin,' the foreman

said clinically. 'We'll lift it off the van onto a trolley by hand. They told you about the customs, did they?'

'Yes.'

Stenski had gone from the van. Johnson opened the rear doors and a workman climbed in and pushed the coffin forward while three others caught it and lowered it onto the trolley. They pushed it through the shed with Johnson walking solemnly behind.

'Normally,' the foreman said, 'We put a sheet over the coffins. People don't like to see that kind of thing, especially at an airport. But at this time of the morning, it's not worth it . . . '

The customs room was an annex, built later than the hangar. They let the advancing trolley thrust the flimsy double doors apart. A customs official sat at a table, reading a book. They left the trolley in the middle of the room. He lifted his peaked cap from a peg on the wall behind him, put it on with some ceremony, adjusted it minutely, and came over.

Johnson already had the papers out and stood at the end of the coffin, a few feet away. The official was tall and, in his little kingdom — a room with no windows, full of official decrees and proclamations and instructions scattered round the brick walls, where his word was, quite literally, law, and his smallest whim important — he was very conscious of his position. He stood erect for a long time, looking now at Johnson, now at the coffin. His uniform was navy blue, and the cap matched it. The jacket was decorated by a row of silver buttons and, about the breast pocket, a green ribbon. It might have been awarded in the War; it might be for long service.

'A coffin,' he observed as he walked across, measuring the steps. 'A high grade coffin, too. That is very good wood.' He surveyed it again from a short distance with the cold eye of a man who had seen a few coffins before.

'My wife,' Johnson said, affecting helplessness. 'I have the certificate of her death here.'

'No doubt.' He came closer. 'You are English, of course.' How the hell did he know that? 'Your accent,' he observed

189

flatly. 'Quite different from all the others.' He looked straight at Johnson. 'Are you transporting the body of your wife to England?'

'No. She was Swedish.'

'I see.' He took the white, thin sheet of paper which Johnson offered to him, surveyed it, and walked back to the table where he sat. Johnson, unsure of what to do, followed. 'The certificate of death,' the official said. He removed his cap and returned it to the peg. He studied the paper for some moments. 'Cardiac arrest?'

'Yes. It happened very suddenly, while I was at work. They found her in the kitchen. I haven't really got myself sorted out yet I'm afraid.' Stenski had been most emphatic: Don't play for sympathy. They don't care about you. But they'll all be trying to help you ... decency will compel that.

'You realise,' the man said, looking up from the paper, 'that the certificate is incorrectly completed?' He pointed towards the bottom of the paper. 'You must have the signature of two qualified doctors. You have only one. See for yourself.'

Johnson was drawn between anger and fear. All that checking Stenski had insisted on, all that mumbo-jumbo about the tie-pins. Johnson felt cold. It's me, he thought bitterly, I'm the one who has to actually do it, facing a man like this. The official shifted his backside on the chair to a more comfortable position. He completed the movement with a flourish to release the coat-tails of his jacket and they hung, in unison, over the edge of the chair, as limp as bat's wings and the same colour.

'I'm very sorry,' Johnson said. The black gloves felt awkward in his hand. 'The doctor was very sympathetic. Austrian doctors are so good.' He searched for the effect of the compliment. There was none. 'But he did not mention this.'

'Perhaps he did and you have forgotten.'

'I don't know if you are married . . . '

You must be helpless, Stenski had said, helpless and lost. Delayed shock. Then whatever you do, they won't find it strange.

'My first wife died during the War,' the official said flatly. 'She was bombed. They did not even search for the body. They told me it was not worth it. I was serving on the Eastern Front at that time. But I came home and made sure that two doctors signed the certificate.' He took out a gold-coloured ball point pen and began to manipulate it gently between his fingers. 'A very difficult situation, I am sure you will agree. Only one signature.' He brought the pen down to just above the paper and held it there. Johnson imagined for one moment that he was going to sign the certificate; but he changed his mind, flicked the top of the pen so that the small ball at its tip was retracted, and clipped it back in his pocket. 'We shall have to open the coffin. Unless you object. There are, of course, qualified doctors at the airport. It would be a simple matter to have one of them examine the body and add their signature. I cannot see that they would object. Otherwise, you will have to take the coffin away and obtain the second signature elsewhere.'

Johnson was squeezing the gloves in his hand. That would be nice, pretty damn nice. The official would summon a doctor, simply undo the eight screws, lift the lid away and see Andrushenko sleeping like a baby, his mouth half open and revealing all those rotten teeth.

'I couldn't bear to see her again.'

'Oh.' He stood up and reached for his cap. 'You could always go out and wait in the other room. It would not take very long, a few minutes.' The official seemed displeased. He walked back to the coffin. The breathing holes were small and bored under the protruding lip of the lid all the way round. They would almost certainly be visible in this room with its high arclamps positioned to aid investigation. He ran his finger along the lid. 'Very good wood,' he observed to nobody in particular. 'The grain is constant on all the sides. Sometimes they make the lids of good quality but not the sides. It must have cost a great deal.'

Johnson went over, shuffling his feet

noisily. Get his eyes off the coffin. 'For Christ's sake,' he almost shouted. 'Don't be so bloody inhuman. My wife is in there.'

The official turned.

'I'm sorry,' Johnson said.

The man wandered round the coffin, satisfied with the apology. He stooped briefly, gazing at one of the side panels. The wall clock moved to nine thirty. 'What,' he mused, 'are we going to do?'

'Surely, when something like this happens you make some allowances?' He was almost sweating. They would insist on opening the coffin. It would be jail. They'd call him a terrorist. Christ, Christ, ten years at least for that. How was he going to begin to explain it all, in a cold and hostile court of law? Kidnap, blackmail, perhaps attempted murder . . . he wanted to scream at the man: Don't keep looking at me like that!

The eyes were blue, chill as the dawn.

The bomb, that's what it was. One dirty little bomb thirty years ago which knocked down some little house somewhere, and the man had never forgiven.

Johnson wanted to spit it at him: What about London, what about Coventry? What about Liverpool, what about Newcastle? and what about the docks at Belfast, what about . . . ?

He said nothing.

It occurred to him at that precise moment, when the panic was rising like a discordant note inside him — and it was odd that the thought had only come to him now — that whatever did happen, whether they opened the coffin or not, Stenski would be all right. He would be in the passenger lounge now, not reading, not drinking, not even sipping a cup of coffee like any normal man, but just sitting there, wrapped up in that old coat. Nobody could touch him. He wasn't even implicated, unless Johnson talked. Stenski was clean. Of course. What did you expect?

The official sat down. 'Your ticket, please, and the receipt from the freight company for the coffin.' The death certificate lay at his elbow, creased in a pattern where it had been folded. 'Passports. Both. Yours, and that of your wife.'

He laid all the documents out in front of him. 'At least they seem in order,' he said. He pulled back a drawer and took from it a metal stamp with a shaped, wooden handle. The varnish had been worn from it over the years. He inked it from a pad, rocking it back and forward several times then pressed it down on the certificate. 'I have given the coffin clearance,' he said. He pressed a bell and the workmen came back. He nodded to them, a controlled, imperious gesture of authority. They wheeled the trolley across to the conveyor belt against a wall: it was low and wide, a succession of chromium rolling bars. They lifted the coffin onto it and the official went to the end of the belt, pulled down a switch on the wall, and the bars began to rotate. The coffin moved forward, bouncing gently as it traversed the bars, and disappeared through the square aperture in the outside wall.

From now on, it would have a life of its own.

Johnson felt only a mingling of relief and doubt. Just like at a cremation.

'I'm sorry about the bomb,' he said stupidly.

'Which bomb?'

'Your wife.'

The man stared at him, mildly astonished that he should have remembered. 'I was told that it happened in broad daylight, early one afternoon,' he said. 'Everybody knows that it was the Americans who bombed during the day, and the English at night. Not that it can matter now. Goodbye.'

Stenski was in the lounge, sitting near the departures board. Flights to Athens, Munich, Stuttgart, Bonn, Milan and Prague were on it, and green boarding lights blinked on and off against the last two.

'You made a mistake,' Johnson said quickly. He had put the gloves in his pocket, but they protruded. 'It could have been a disastrous mistake. In Austria you need two doctor's signatures on a death certificate, not one. We only had one.' Stenski was not particularly impressed. 'The customs officer wanted to unscrew the lid and have a look. That was a compassionate little touch, wasn't it? Now you tell me what would have happened the moment the lid came off?'

'I have never cared for speculation,' Stenski said. 'You should know that.' He cleared his throat with a forced cough. 'It was, however, most instructive.' He was in his worst, superior mood. 'The law, of course, was changed here some years ago. You do not need two doctors to tell you that one man is dead. It is hardly possible that this customs official was not acquainted with the regulations.'

'Then why all the fuss?'

'I have already told you. They are stupid. They try a little ruse like that to pass the time, then they got bored with it, put their hoofmark on all the pieces of paper and go back to sleep.'

Johnson knew that Stenski was lying. He had lied before, but only when it was necessary. And at those moments, he had lied regardless of the effect on their relationship. He couldn't have known anything about the regulations.

'Next time,' Johnson said crisply, 'you

go and see how stupid they are. I want a drink.'

★ ★ ★

The plane was only ten minutes late taking off. They sat at opposite sides of the corridor and far apart again. Stenski imagined that that would be more secure. He slept, as he habitually did on aeroplanes, for want of anything better to do, his lean head pushed back against the rest and turned to one side.

Johnson looked down at his hands. Grains of sugar were in the folds of the skin. His tie was loose. He felt sticky and uncomfortable.

They landed at Copenhagen shortly before one o'clock. The terminal building might have been anywhere; even the shops along the middle of it were conventional, selling food, and alcohol, and boxes of cigars; and toys, and small trinkets which people bore away in sealed green carrier bags.

Johnson found a bar, a curved counter with fixed stools at intervals around it.

The barman wore a white shirt with the sleeves rolled up to the elbows, and spoke sporadic English. Johnson ordered a beer. Stenski disliked stools and sat in a chair at a table nearby.

'What about lunch? You slept through the meal on the plane,' Johnson asked loudly.

'A sandwich, that's all I want. A meat sandwich.'

'We don't serve sandwiches here,' the barman said. 'You have to go up to the cafeteria.'

Stenski went by himself to a long room on another level, collected a metal tray and joined the queue shuffling along. The girl on the till was young. He paid in dollars, and she gave him change in Danish money, a few odd coins with holes in the middle. Stenski kept them as a matter of principle. He carried the sandwiches back downstairs and ate them on the table. Johnson was drinking another beer.

Forty minutes before the flight was due to leave, Stenski began to become agitated. 'They should have called it by now,' he said and walked to the departures board. It was up there, in the moving, white letters which clatter as they rotate and stop to form a flight number and a destination. The green lights were blinking against flights after theirs. Against Stockholm, there was nothing. He came back and positioned himself at the far side of the table. The cellophane in which the sandwiches had been wrapped lay crumpled in front of him. 'Why don't they make an announcement?' He looked at the barman. Those people always seem to know things like that. 'I expect some silly girl has got it wrong. Pressed the wrong button.' He could find nothing to console him, sat down and looked in the direction of the departures board again.

The announcement did come, a quarter of an hour later in a distorted voice over the tannoy, recited in Danish, Swedish and English: 'Scandinavian Airlines regret that flight 743 to Stockholm is delayed because of weather conditions.' That was all. Stenski immediately went off in search of the airline information desk. A pretty girl with blonde, straight

201

hair and a cap, said: 'It is fog. There is fog over most of the Baltic. You will be informed by announcement when there is any further news.'

Stenski was going to be dogmatic about it. Johnson could see that, even from where he sat at the bar. 'How long will it be? I have a business appointment and it is very important. Can you ring somebody and ask the length of the delay?'

'There is no point,' she said. 'They will inform us.'

He returned to the table, sat again. Johnson joined him. Stenski was counting: 'Six o'clock is the maximum. The injection lasts for 15 hours. It is now' — and he glanced at his watch — '2.27. The flying time is almost two hours from here. Stockholm is further north than one might imagine. That means that we must take off by four at the latest.'

'He'll start to wake up at six,' Johnson said dully. 'That will be the moment we land, if we take off at four.' He lifted the glass towards his mouth but the circular paper mat stuck to its base and he disengaged it with difficulty. 'My mouth is so dry. Dry as the bottom of a birdcage.'

Stenski was looking at his watch again.

'I wonder where the coffin is now?' Johnson said. 'In some transit area, I suppose.'

Stenski was examining options in the secretive way he had. He had returned to the information desk. The girl had gone. Another, equally blonde, had taken her place. 'SAS 743,' Stenski said without preliminaries.

She consulted a screen in front of her. 'Delayed,' she said pleasantly. 'Delayed indefinitely.'

That was what angered him most: The blank, thoughtless mouthing of information. 'Can you find out how long?' He held his hat in his hand and brushed it against his leg in impatience.

She didn't want to co-operate. She had the created, unmoving smile and curt manner which comes, inescapably, from dealing with people. 'It won't do any good,' she said. She began to press buttons on the keyboard on the screen. From where he stood, he could not see what the result was. She was unable, or unwilling, to do more.

'What is the forecast? Is there no Met. Office?'

'They only tell us what time the flights leave. We just repeat what we are told.'

He grunted. Some Americans were pushing behind him and one clutched an enormous tartan coloured suitcase plastered with garish labels. Stenski turned and looked at them in disgust. He strode back to Johnson. 'They know nothing,' Stenski said. 'Nothing at all.'

'Nice looking girl?' Johnson was drifting easily towards drunkenness. 'At least Andrushenko got nearer than us. If he'd resisted the tablet a few minutes more, he'd have had that girl. A little bit of good, honest decadence.' He laughed stupidly.

Stenski ignored him and concentrated on his watch. 2.45. 'What is so special about a bit of fog?' He had his hands locked together as if they were in supplication before the fact. 'In the war . . .'

'I don't think I can take much more,'

Johnson said, the serious posture of the drunk. 'Really, I mean that. Know what I mean? In the customs this morning, with that bastard quizzing me and messing me about, I nearly wet myself. No way to live.' He drank from the glass and closed his eyes. He heard movement, felt Stenski's coat brush against him, and opened his eyes. Stenski was going back to the information counter. The girl shook her head, then, from below the counter, lifted a telephone and spoke into it, smiled and said something to Stenski.

'Soon,' he said to Johnson when he came back.

It was three. 'How long is the drive from the airport at Stockholm?' Johnson asked. 'If we take off at half past three, we arrive at half past five. That only leaves thirty minutes.'

'Clearly, we will have to stop on the way,' Stenski said. He looked disapprovingly at the glass in Johnson's hand. 'We will have to buy tools and open the coffin the moment we get clear of the airport. If he suffocates, that spoils everything.'

'But you said the holes were big enough.'

'For a sleeping man. For a man asleep. In that case, respiration is significantly lower. When he wakes up . . . '

Johnson went to the bar and ordered a coffee. It was too brown and strong, almost acrid. He put a lot of sugar in to soften the taste.

'You realise you have to drive when we get there,' Stenski said.

'Meaning what?'

Stenski was looking at his watch.

They called the flight at three fifteen. The green boarding light and the announcement came at the same moment. Stenski stood up and Johnson said: 'Gate fourteen.' They went back down the long corridors to a waiting room and had their tickets checked. Seventy or eighty other passengers were in the room. A green and yellow leafed rubber plant spread up and out from a barrel which had been sawn in half. Cigarettes had been stubbed out in the reddish soil in which it stood. They moved down a gangway when the stewardess summoned them and through a hatch onto the plane itself.

When they were in the air, Johnson wondered if they should not have enquired about the coffin: Ensured that transfer from Austrian Airlines had gone smoothly. He relapsed. That was Stenski's problem.

He woke as they were landing. They were coming down the stairway when Stenski said: 'It's five thirty already.'

'What if he wakes and starts shouting? That would be the natural reaction. He'll start clawing the sides.'

'Precisely. I have been turning that over in my mind while you have been asleep.' It was a reproach. 'This is what we must do: I will collect both our suitcases while you go off and organise the van. It should be waiting. It must be waiting.'

'What if you are stopped by the customs carrying my suitcase?'

'Most unlikely. This is Sweden. Very lax like that.'

'Better to stick together,' Johnson said. 'We'll get the luggage and be through in a moment. Otherwise we'll lose each other. We've never been here before. We don't even know the layout of the airport.'

Stenski looked at his watch again; it had become almost a mannerism. Johnson had an unmistakable hangover. A dull headache was beginning behind his temples. They waited together beside the circular conveyor belt where the luggage would come, Stenski becoming increasingly impatient. The other passengers grouped themselves at its rim. 'Where is it? These people can't organise anything.'

Johnson told him to calm down.

'Five forty two.' Stenski pointed to a hanging clock, suspended by two metal bars from the ceiling for confirmation. A porter came.

'Any minute now,' Johnson said.

The luggage was spewed up from a gap in the dome round which the conveyor belt run, fell away onto the belt itself and began to circle the dome; hands were thrust forward, and lifted them off.

'That's mine,' Johnson said.

Stenski could not see his, and was on the point of abandoning it altogether and leaving without it.

'Don't be silly,' Johnson said.

The old leather case did come, then, alone, towards the end of the consignment. Stenski seized it without thought and they tramped through the Nothing to Declare avenue in the customs. An official gazed at them distantly as they went by, but wasn't interested. Outside, Johnson asked for the Hertz desk. It was downstairs, and they used the escalator. A man was running it.

'Speak English?' Johnson asked.

He nodded.

'Look, we're in a terrible hurry.' Stenski stood at his shoulder, listening, poised to intervene.

'A van. In the name of Henderson.'

'Yes. To be collected. Passport and driver's licence, please.'

Johnson laid them on the counter. Henderson: A comfortable English name which he had used before. He had all the papers in that name, too. No problems.

The man looked briefly at the passport, made Johnson sign two pieces of paper, told him the registration number and gave him the keys. 'It is in the car park,' he said. 'The colour is yellow. The registration number is also printed on the disc, in case you forget it.' He indicated the small, blue circular disc attached to the keyring.

Stenski said loudly: 'Five fifty. We had better go.' He still held the old suitcase as if, by placing it on the ground, he might waste time.

They walked as fast as they decently could out of some plate-glass doors. It had grown suddenly dark and cold.

'Over there,' Johnson said. There were six vans in a corner. Johnson found theirs and unlocked the door. They both climbed in. It was maddening how the controls on every vehicle in the world were in different places. He couldn't find the side lights; they sprang on suddenly, and he wasn't even sure which switch had done it. The headlamps came on full beam, illuminating the parked cars away into the distance. He struggled to find the dip-switch. He turned the ignition on, but where was reverse? Did he have to push the gear stick down, or lift it up? He felt the mesh in the gear box catch it, and they backed out, turned and headed off towards the freight area.

'Five forty six.' Stenski was peering at his watch.

'Spare me the running commentary,' Johnson said.

The freight area was better organised than Vienna; and more modern, with a reception bureau.

'Flight SAS 743,' Johnson said to the man there. 'It's a coffin.'

'They would have brought that off last. They put them in a special compartment.'

'I know.'

The man went to a black telephone on the wall and made a short call. 'It is in the customs now.' He noticed Johnson's black suit and tie. He had lost the gloves somewhere back out there. Stenski was at his shoulder again. They stood at the end of the room and watched the doors at the other end, waiting.

'Probably it won't be exactly six when he comes out of it,' Johnson said, seeking comfort.

'It could easily have been before,' Stenski said. 'I have thought of that. He would be dead now. Silent and dead.'

'He might be alive and out of it too. That's a hell of a thought. Remember the coffin is in my name.'

'I think only this: If he came out of it on the aeroplane, he certainly will be dead. We must draw a measure of comfort from that. Nobody would have heard him above the noise of the engines. If he is still alive, we shall put that down to good management.'

The minute hand on the wall clock moved in a single, jerking movement to five fifty eight. The doors were pushed open, and a small electric tractor towed the coffin on a trailer. 'You'll have to sign for it,' the man said. Johnson scribbled the name Henderson on a docket.

'Can you take it outside? We have a van.'

'Of course.'

The tractor continued down the wide corridor and they hurried after it. Stenski had a way of walking so that he could accelerate without altering the posture of his body.

The man summoned assistance, and they lifted the coffin into the opened rear of the van, sliding it until it was within in the door. Stenski had resumed his seat. Johnson watched the workmen. When he had locked the doors, he felt obliged to tip them. He had no Swedish money, so he gave them an American dollar each.

'No good here,' the driver of the tractor observed, holding the note in his hand.

'You can change it.'

'Don't get involved,' Stenski called back. He was already settled, his coat gathered around him. 'Tell them to go away.'

Johnson made a helpless gesture with both hands. The workman thrust the bank note into his trouser pocket without troubling to fold it, and walked away.

'Tools,' Stenski said. 'Stop at the first garage.'

'We have no money,' Johnson replied. 'If they won't accept dollars as a tip at an airport, I don't fancy our chances of actually buying things with them.'

'I have some Swedish kroner. Quite enough for some elementary tools.'

'Why didn't you say before?'

'I do not approve of tipping. If you are paid as a porter, you are paid as a porter. Why should I contribute more?'

They were out on the road now, a dual carriageway lit by orange lamps on tall concrete standards.

'Just drive towards Stockholm,' Stenski said. Johnson scanned the roadside for a garage. Six nine. 'It is important when we find one,' Stenski said, 'that we do not speak so we do not reveal who we are or where we have come from.' He had recovered his poise, and was putting himself at a distance from Johnson again. 'I shall do it.'

They found a petrol station the other side of a place called Solna. In the darkness, there was so much neon that, even from a short distance, it looked like a gin palace. Johnson avoided the line of pumps and parked away from the main building, positioning the van in the shadows. Stenski got out and walked quickly back. He went in. The man at the cash desk was reading. Motor accessories filled the whole of the centre of the room.

Shelves and racks were stacked with

214

them. Beyond, a lorry driver in blue overalls sipped coffee from a beaker he had just taken from the vending machine. Stenski hunted among the accessories. He did not drive, and he had never driven. He had not imagined that anybody would want to manufacture so many gadgets for motor vehicles, or could find a market for them. The tool kits were at the back in clear plastic bags: Forty kroner. He lifted one off the hook and took it to the cash desk, held it up so that the man could see the price, and counted out four ten kroner notes.

Johnson still had the engine running.

'Turn off into a side road. Somewhere dark and quiet,' Stenski said. He had already prised the neck of the plastic bag open and his long fingers were gauging the shape of the tools.

'A screw-driver?'

'Of course a screw-driver. I would not have purchased the tool kit otherwise.'

They were out in the country on a straight road headed towards Enkoping.

'Not much traffic in Sweden,' Johnson observed. The headlights licked the road, picking out the sign: Lassa 1 KM. 'It's out of our way, but that doesn't matter.' They turned left off the main road into a narrow lane. Beyond the grass verges, Johnson could see conifer trees. 'I'll pull off here,' he said, indicating a gateway which opened into a field.

Tractors had used the gateway, and the ground was uneven. The van bounced crazily as Johnson backed it up between the gate posts. He switched the head-lamps off and they sat in darkness. Away to the left they could see a single row of white street lights. 'That must be Lassa,' Johnson said. 'Only a village.' Stenski handed him the screw-driver. He clambered between the two front seats, and Stenski pressed himself against the door to give him space to get through. 'We'll have to have the interior light on,' Johnson said when he was crouched over the coffin. 'I can't see a thing.'

'Most insecure. Use a match. I have a box here.'

'Don't be absurd.'

Stenski hesitated, then conceded. He couldn't find the switch for the interior light. Johnson came back, groped for it, and couldn't find it either. 'The thing comes on when you open the door,' he said. 'When I get back near the coffin, just open your door a little.'

'You are behaving very foolishly,' Stenski said. 'Not what I have come to expect. And I do not discount the quantity you drank at the airport at Copenhagen. Your conduct there was almost irresponsible. The police here are very strict about that kind of thing: Drinking and driving.'

'If you want a row, just say so. I've never seen a van like this before, I have no idea where the controls are — but I am expected to jump straight into it, and drive it flat out at night, then work in total darkness with a screw-driver. Sorry. Not total darkness. With a match in one hand.'

'Six twenty three,' Stenski said.

'So open the door a little, all right?'

As the door swung back, the interior light did come on.

'That's better.'

Eight screws, each one sunk into a small cavity; each demanding pressure from the elbow and wrist before they could be drawn upward. As each loosened, he finished unscrewing it with his fingers, stored it in his trouser pocket. He had to remove all eight before the lid could be pushed away. He peered down into the coffin. Andrushenko was still asleep. He had not moved. His arms were at his sides, his feet close together, one shoe resting on the other. He looked cold — his skin had turned a sour, creamy colour — but he was still breathing.

Johnson looked up. Stenski was sitting erect in the front seat, staring through the windscreen into the night.

'Don't you even want to see?' Johnson was astonished.

'If he is dead, that only makes things a little more complicated. If he is alive . . . '

The sweat was running down Johnson's forehead as he squatted at the far end of the coffin. He brushed it away with the sleeve of his coat. 'What are we going to do? We can't just leave him like this. He is going to wake up sometime, after all.' Still Stenski did not move.

Johnson's feet were on the coconut

matting which covered the floor of the van. He shuffled them forward and Stenski did turn then.

'What are we going to do?'

'Secure his hands, replace the lid, but not screw it down. Then drive to our destination,' Stenski said.

'Of course, of course, of course.' Johnson had raised his voice again, but now imitating a woman. It was his way of taunting Stenski.

'Secure his hands. Why didn't I think of that?'

'I cannot imagine,' Stenski said. He understood the intonation in Johnson's voice clearly enough, but disregarded it.

'There is a problem, of course,' Johnson went on as if Stenski had not even answered. He maintained the voice. 'We have nothing to secure his hands with. Or am I becoming too technical?'

'You do not imagine I would spend a great deal of money on a tool kit without first ascertaining whether it included a tow rope. The label on the bag is printed in several languages. The manufacturers claim that the breaking-strain is sufficient

219

to pull a caravan. I imagine it will be strong enough to secure his hands. We could have employed a tie, as he did with the woman. I thought you might have suggested that. However' — and he coughed; the door was still ajar, and the night air was reaching his chest — 'use the tow rope.' His hand was in the plastic bag again, drawing it out.

Johnson took the coil of straw-coloured rope. He was thankful Andrushenko was thin; he had enough space inside the coffin to turn him onto his back, fold his limp arms across his chest, and tie the wrists together. He had a rudimentary knowledge of knots and remembered, distantly, a couple of the names: Clovehitch, sheepshank. He'd forgotten the rest. There was a time, when he was not yet ten and had stood in the scout hut every Monday evening in short trousers and wearing a cap, when he could do them all, the clovehitch, the sheepshank, and plenty more besides. Now, with Andrushenko's chill flesh in his hands — both the textures of the skin, and the hairs on it repelled him — he was only concerned about the right tension.

Not too slack, not too taut. The rope was coated in something hard and clear; water-proofing, he supposed. Worse, it wasn't pliable at all, and he had to create a large, ungainly knot around the wrists.

'That should do,' he said. He climbed back into the driving seat, and Stenski closed his door. They drove in silence to the main road, and went north.

'I have memorised the route,' Stenski remarked, after the silence had been prolonged so long that it had become artificial. 'We turn towards Veckholm soon.'

'These vans are nothing like cars to handle,' Johnson said as pleasantly as he could. It was his way of altering the atmosphere between them. He glanced across. 'Aren't you happy? All right, it was a bit hairy, I'll admit that, in Vienna. But it was me, you see, it was me taking all the risks. That's all.'

'You were not obliged to come,' Stenski replied. He had not altogether accepted the apology.

Johnson ignored that. 'I feel like a good meal.'

'We shall not eat tonight. In the morning, you can go and buy provisions. You can also telephone McClellan and report our safe arrival. He will be anxious for news. You will pose as a tourist. The place where we are going is sparsely populated, but it overlooks a lake. Foreigners will be unremarkable there.'

'In December?'

'I am told so. The Scandinavians value that kind of thing, fresh air, keeping fit, cross-country skiing. I am sure they will swim in the lake. Unless it is iced over, of course. These Scandinavians, who are so superior and are forever holding them-selves up as the moral guardians of the world: What right have they? I have never been here of course, but I am told that, during the War, they turned Norwegians back at the frontier when they were trying to escape from the Germans. Other people have told me that at weekends whole towns get drunk then fight each other. A woman even recounted to me how, in the far north, they put their hands into electric plugs and light sockets because the shock gives them some kind of pleasure. We had better be careful here if there are such basic contradictions in their character.'

'Was it really necessary to come to Sweden?'

'I tried to visualise it from every position. In Berlin, I walked at night, examining it from three or four stand-points — while you were dealing with Mr. Barnard. I did not concern myself with what we think. I tried to imagine what they would think.'

'And . . . '

'If you were Andrushenko, and you decided to defect, where would you elect to go? America? Perhaps, but you are going to have to like the American way of life, and the CIA people have a reputation for getting things wrong. Britain? Too small now. West Germany? A Russian is hardly going to want to go there, especially if he has a War record. And, in any case, what if he defected for other reasons? Supposing he didn't want to sell what he knew, but only live peacefully somewhere — and not alone? That is the premise.'

The road looped. The white line which had run down its middle was gone; the cat's eyes were gone, too, and there was nothing to guide the driver except the grass verges; the pine trees were dark in the night, blending into a wall which could not be penetrated.

'Here is a man whose value is what he knows. He may choose to sell it to the highest bidder. What does he do? He does not go to America or Britain or West Germany, because that would be delivering himself into the enemy camp. He would be robbed of his bargaining power. He selects a neutral country — Sweden, a country which has proclaimed itself neutral irrespective of what the rest of the community of nations may think of it for doing so. Once inside that country — a country, let us not forget, with no extradition treaties, and the profoundest regard for human deserters of all kinds — he puts out feelers. To our side, he has knowledge to sell. To his own side, he has silence to sell. He can hardly fail. Indeed, if a man were shrewd enough, he might make both buy.'

Stenski caressed an idea he alone had created.

'He must know a great deal,' Stenski continued. 'A greater part of his life has been spent in intelligence work. Thirty years of it. If he chose to sing, he would sing a very interesting song.'

'But it would be untypical. You said it yourself: Thirty years devoted service to the cause, or whatever they call it. And suddenly one fine day, he flies away.'

'You do not understand them. The Russians keep smiling, just like the East Germans — a protective smile, as fixed as a mask and maintained so that nobody knows what they are thinking. That is why, at a personal level, they are never trusted. They know that a man can live comfortably behind his mask for years if he needs to, and all the time he is calculating how to get away . . . when the border guards will be off balance, how to traverse the minefield, how far the beams from the searchlights carry. Whether it would be better to make his run on a Monday morning or a Wednesday evening. You have seen some of the defectors, and what are they? Not just a handful of teenagers, lured by the neon on the other side, dreaming of the freedom to watch pornographic films — but doctors, who have built up solid practices, factory managers with good salaries, the ones who might have been expected to stay.'

Johnson slowed the van as the road began to twist and turn.

'Nobody will be particularly surprised that Andrushenko decided to go, and nobody will be surprised that he chose the right moment: After a party, in a foreign country, when the only man with him had had a lot to drink. That would be his right moment. Sweden would be the natural choice: Safe, neutral to a nauseating degree, packed with welfare workers waving white flags.'

They reached a cross-road and turned north again, on the Borlange road. They came into the snow the other side of a deserted town which, according to the signpost, was called Sala. Stenski had not heard of it, and was mystified for a moment. The snow was not like Austria: It was dry and sharp, lying in patches at first, each fringed by grey ice. Soon it deepened into banks against the trees. Twenty kilometres further on, the trees had gone and they were into the tundra. The wind skimmed the surface of the snow, lifting and spreading it in powder, like a sandstorm; and moaned across a wasteland of smooth rock and lichen.

Johnson slowed further. Snow lay on the road itself, drifting in the wind and pushing at the windscreen of the van, leaving a melted film of water upon it. He switched the wipers on.

And still Andrushenko did not wake. The lid lay against the side of the coffin, and they could see his feet, unmoving.

Half an hour later, they reached the lake. The moon was up, and its light reflected on the snow. It ran down to the lakeside, where the ice began. Further out, where the ice flow ended and the grey water moved in a constant swell, small waves beat against the rim of the ice, breaking in spurs of white foam. Low, running hills spread out on the far side of the lake, covered in trees.

The road followed the edge of the lake for two kilometres.

'Left,' Stenski said. They turned off onto a track as the road veered away from the lake, and followed that. The house stood on a promitory, gaunt and unlit, looking over the water. The track had become a path of shingle, brought up from the beach, its surface ground down into two equidistant ruts by the vehicles which had used it before. Johnson parked by the front door.

'The keys were posted on to me,' Stenski said. He was peering at the house. It was made entirely of wood, probably pine, in the form of planks arranged vertically. All four front windows were concealed behind closed shutters; one was loose, and vibrated noisily in the wind.

Johnson looked towards the coffin. 'Still asleep.'

'I have considered that, also. The doctor gave me the minimum time, just as one would expect a doctor to do. They always cover themselves like that. The maximum time may be quite different.'

*   *   *

Barnard found a hotel and asked himself if he should ring McClellan and get clearance to go on. There was something about that which disturbed him, something about the under-secretary from the Embassy who had come to visit him in hospital: He had actually mentioned McClellan's name, so he must have spoken to him. And McClellan had wanted him taken off it. The Embassy man would never have dared invent that.

McClellan, obviously, had got frightened when the violence started. A nervous pansy. A clerk behind a desk.

But could he go on by himself, in spite of McClellan and in spite of instructions? There may have been other reasons why McClellan wanted him taken off it, reasons which Barnard knew nothing about. Obedience was the primary rule. Just like the Army. Thinking soldiers are not encouraged. If they think, they'll

make their own judgements, start dis-
agreeing.

He climbed off the bed and had a
shower. It was nine, and he felt hungry.
He ate in the restaurant downstairs and
slept ten hours afterwards.

\* \* \*

Stenski stood at the bedroom door. He
was still wearing his hat and coat. 'I will
spend the night here with him,' he
announced. 'You bring the suitcases in
then go to sleep.' Stenski unbuttoned the
coat, moved to the end of the bed, and sat
down. Andrushenko lay on his side up the
bed, hands bound in front of him.
Johnson had removed his shoes and
placed them side by side under the bed. 'I
wish to be present when he wakes,'
Stenski said, settling like a crow on its
nest.

Johnson camped down in the bedroom
opposite. It was cold. An old grate was
sunk into one wall, but he would have
needed coal or logs for that, and there
was neither. Across the passage, Stenski

had turned on the bedside light. Johnson could picture him perfectly, the predator, careless of time and hunger, careless of fatigue. His bony fingers would be locked together on his lap. His shoes would be perfectly clean.

Johnson felt his anxieties fall away from him once he had drawn the old duvet over himself, and he seemed to be tumbling down through layers of darkness. The day retreated into memory. He gave himself up to sleep.

Snow was falling when he woke; he could sense it in the air, and when he opened the shutters thick flakes were descending as slowly as the leaves of autumn. He surveyed the lake. Nothing moved on it, no boat, no bird, except the water out beyond the ice. The hills were further away than he thought. He looked left and right along the shore, searching for other houses. He couldn't see any. He closed the shutters and went into the other bedroom.

Andrushenko was awake. He had not moved. Stenski was standing, his back to the wall. He had placed his hat on the end of the bed, near Andrushenko's feet. For a long time, nobody spoke.

Then Stenski said: 'He woke three hours ago. He speaks nothing but Russian, except a few Ukranian words of abuse. He understands a respectable amount of German. He wanted to go to the toilet. It was most awkward. I almost woke you. We shall have to consider that in more detail later. We will need a procedure for the toilet.'

Andrushenko murmured something very softly.

'He had deduced that we are English,' Stenski said. 'It was inevitable, of course. It can hardly help him now.'

'But what about afterwards, when it's over?'

'We shall simply deny the whole thing,' Stenski said. 'Nobody could prove anything — and one imagines the Russians will be less than anxious to admit publicly that one of their best men has been taken like this.' He looked down at Andrushenko, who had turned his head away and closed his eyes. 'We have everything we require to press it home to a successful conclusion: Time and solitude. Soon, we shall entertain his friend.'

'And then . . . ?' Johnson had come right into the room. 'It's afterwards that you won't discuss.'

'We shall go away. What could be pleasanter than that? You will be given a new posting, I have no doubt. Perhaps it will be somewhere warm this time.' He wandered casually towards the bed. 'We have certain details to attend to this morning: McClellan must be rung, food must be bought. It will be necessary to conceal the coffin somewhere. There may be an outhouse nearby. If not, I recommend that you break it into small pieces. Perhaps we could use them as fuel for one of these fires.' Stenski gave him 300 kroner in notes, and dismissed him with a nod of the head.

'What are you going to do while I am away?'

'Observe him. I shall allow him the leisure to reflect on his situation; his absolute dependence upon me, for food, for warmth, for the toilet even; perhaps, and he must calculate this also, his life itself.' Stenski seemed content.

'It's a vendetta, isn't it, between you and Markov?'

Stenski did not reply. He contemplated the body on the bed. 'He will come to me.' Whether it was Andrushenko or Markov was not clear.

Johnson dragged the coffin round to the back of the house, went back and carried the lid under his arm. He heaped branches over it and left it until the afternoon.

He drove for an hour and quarter until he reached the nearest town. Just before he reached it, he saw children in a line on their narrow, cross-country skis, following their teacher. They pushed with their legs, steadied themselves with their poles as they struggled across a field deep in snow.

The town was held in the grip of winter. Hardened heaps of snow had been cleared from the pavements and piled against walls; morose eyes scanned him from under brown fur hats, with flaps buttoned down over the ears. He parked the car in a square surrounded by tall buildings. An open air market had been set up: Two rows of canvas stalls selling fruit and vegetables, shirts and toys, assorted domestic goods. He wandered over. For the first time for days, he felt no particular urgency.

A huge, forlorn man wearing soiled white fur boots and a heavy beard, his face ravaged by the weather, shuffled to and fro behind a trestle table, trying to keep warm. He cupped his raw hands, brought them to his mouth and breathed heavily into them. Around him, draped over transverse wire, he had arranged pelts and skins. Women stopped and examined them, pressing the thin strips of hide between thumb and forefinger to gauge the quality; but nobody was buying. He was a Sami tribesman, no doubt, from the far north.

Johnson found a hamburger caravan where a young girl was serving.

'Do you speak English?'

She nodded coyly. People stirred, hearing the foreign words, and she was obviously embarrassed.

'Is there a post office near here?'

She didn't understand 'post office'.

'A place to telephone?' He mimicked making a telephone call with his hands and arms. She giggled.

'Over there,' she said. She pointed out through the bare trees which fringed the square.

It was on the ground floor of one of the buildings. A woman sat in a glass cubicle near the door, and he wrote the number on a piece of paper, pushed it through the grille towards her. She looked at it and he stood while she dialled. A ball of wool and knitting needles lay on her lap; from the half-completed carcass of wool, he deduced that she was making a child's pullover. When she had finished dialling, she listened for a long time, then said something in Swedish. He shook his head. 'Cabin one,' she said in English motioning towards it.

Inside, he lifted the receiver. 'London?'

'Yes.' The voice seemed distant and flattened.

'McClellan, please.'

'Hold on. I'm putting you through.'

There was a pause. At least the line was tolerable.

'McClellan here.'

'We arrived safely, all three of us. Nothing more yet.'

'Where are you speaking from?'

'A post office.'

'Why are you not using the Embassy telex?'

'He told me to ring.'

'Oh.' McClellan sounded less than happy.

'It's too far to the Embassy, anyway.'

'All right. Try and use the telex in future.'

'It's very secure here. I'm right out in the sticks. A little town at the back of beyond.'

'No transit problems?'

'No.'

'Good.'

'It's bloody cold here.'

'Never mind the weather reports.'

'Sorry.' Johnson had never known McClellan well, spoke only occasionally to him, and each time found it awkward. 'Any news from Berlin?'

'Nothing. That case has been closed. It is not important now.'

'Any message for me to take back?'

'Tell him to keep up the good work. We're all behind him. That's all.'

'OK.'

Johnson put the receiver down, paid the woman, who had already written the cost on the back of his piece of paper, and went back to the market to buy food.

It was curious how much shorter the journey back seemed to be. As he came out of the town, he slowed, searching for the children. That was what he had been denied all these years: The normality, the children, the breathing of cold air, the teasing and joking; the open fire at night, with the smell of hot food flowing from the kitchen.

But the children had gone.

He thought about Berlin. He wondered what had happened there for Barnard to be taken off it. Case Closed. That was what McClellan had said. Case Closed. He had been emphatic. And McClellan always picked his words. But why? Johnson couldn't understand it at all.

When he reached the house, Stenski was in the kitchen.

'Any progress?' Johnson asked.

'It will take a while. He does not seem a martyr. That, at least, is a beginning. It is only a question of applying the correct pressure, and he will break up like the ice on the lake. I have been looking at the lake while you have been away, how odd it is, something beyond our kind of world, chill and uncharted, like the country itself; uncounted trees, the endless rock. It must have a very depressing effect upon the inhabitants.' They went to the bedroom together. Andrushenko remained in the same position. It must have been uncomfortable for him to lie on his back. Stenski asked him, a short, pointed sentence what he wanted to eat. 'He says he does not care. In that case, he will eat what we eat.' As they went out, he added: 'I really am surprised how much Russian I remember.'

Sure, Johnson thought. You've got that kind of memory, the retentive sort. I bet all those irregular Russian verbs are still in there somewhere, filed for future reference. I bet the vocabulary is still in there, too, and not just the common words.

'Go and cook something, Paul. Anything you want.'

'What are we going to do, hand feed him?'

'Since there are two of us here and he is not particularly strong, we shall untie him. That would solve the problem of the food, and also the toilet. He wanted to go again while you were away, but I told him he had to wait. It is all very difficult. He must have a very weak bladder, because he has drunk nothing.'

The wind had begun again; it would be there all winter, as constant as the cold. After a long time, Stenski said: 'I have decided that we will keep his hands tied behind his back. Security apart, the discomfort will encourage him to co-operate. I do not preclude the possibility that we shall have to employ more extreme methods.'

'How extreme?'

'If you are squeamish, you can sit in the van until it's over. I don't mind.' He paused again. 'The lake. Do you find it beautiful? You must tell me.'

'What has that got to do with anything?' Johnson was busy opening tins. The cooker was warming up.

'When I look at it, I am driven to reflect how small an impression man had made. There it is, thousands of years after its creation, hollowed, doubtless, by the retreating ice age, quite untouched. When we have gone from here, we will leave no trace, and it will remain.'

Johnson was not sure he understood what Stenski was saying. Stenski stirred, settled once more into his stance.

'That is why I am indifferent to Andrushenko,' Stenski said. 'Against the grandeur and history of the lake, what does he amount to?'

'And Markov?'

Stenski did not reply.

★　★　★

Barnard booked the call from his bedroom, and lay languidly for two hours waiting for it to come through. The operator was very apologetic. 'There is a two hour delay on all connections with East Berlin,' she said.

He summoned the page boy and told him to go out and buy a shirt, some underclothing a toothbrush and paste, a razor and some blades, shaving cream.

'What size for the shirt?' the boy enquired.

Barnard stood up. 'My size.'

The boy had returned before the call came through.

'Schlidow 29 27 03?' Barnard asked.

'One moment please. I am connecting you now,' the operator said.

'Schlidow 29 27 03?' Barnard repeated.

An infirm, aged woman said 'yes' and wondered who was speaking.

'A friend of Mr. Atkins.'

'Who?'

'Never mind. Eva knew him very well. I have news for her. Can you give her a message?'

'Yes. But she won't be here until tonight. Sometimes she comes back very late.'

'Just tell her a friend of Mr. Atkins has some news. Do you understand? Tell her I will meet her in The Happy Labourer tomorrow at lunch time. One o'clock. I will be by the door.'

'Yes, but who is speaking?'

'It does not matter. She will understand.' The line was very bad.

The old woman muttered something and the line went dead.

\* \* \*

Night came early in the north, stealing into the sombre afternoon like a thief. And Stenski was a creature of the darkness, moving silently round the echoing, wooden house. But it was true that the wind masked sound. It came off the lake, dragging the snow with it; battered against the shutters in eternal yearning.

Stenski had begun to feed Andrushenko baked beans with a spoon, but soon tired of it and, after summoning Johnson to stand by the door, untied his hands and let him feed himself with a fork. 'He will not be allowed a knife at any stage,' Stenski said. The Russian looked dishevelled after three days in the same clothing, unwashed and unshaven. While he ate, Stenski skirted the edge of the bed, watching him. 'Tie his hands again.' Andrushenko had timidly lain the empty plate on the floor. He neither objected nor assisted as Johnson made another knot, but sank back onto the bed and closed his eyes again.

'An obstinate man,' Stenski observed when he came down and they were both in the kitchen. 'I have given him a choice. I have told him that I cannot waste any more time. I have told him, further, that he is making a very bad impression by ignoring all my questions. I have assured him we will use physical means. I have given him an ultimatum: He has thirty minutes to decide. That may seem too long, but psychologically, it is perfect. Let him brood, let him become anxious. He will do that all by himself.'

'What if he doesn't sing the song?'

Stenski checked his watch and went to the window. 'There is a flock of birds on the lake,' he said. 'You see how instinct draws them to the water. They are spread out across the ice.' Johnson joined him.

They were geese, and the wind ruffled their plumage. At that moment, they took to the wing.

After that, Stenski stood alone for a long time. He lifted Johnson's box of matches, placed near the gas cannister, and put them in his pocket. 'We shall go up together, Paul.'

As they went into the bedroom, Andrushenko opened his eyes.

Stenski positioned himself at the end of the bed, so that Andrushenko was looking up at his full height.

'Decision?'

Andrushenko did not speak. His eyes seemed glazed and tired.

'Decision?'

The Russian shook his head. The meaning was clear. He wasn't interested.

Stenski moved round until he stood level with his head. 'Do you want to be blind?' He went to the window, unclipped the heavy metal bar which secured the shutters, and pushed them both open. The wind caught them and dragged them back against the outside wall of the house. At the same moment, it caught the tail of Stenski's coat and twisted it. He forced the frame which held the window pane back down. The room was very still.

'Have a last look,' Stenski said. The daylight was ebbing away. He came back to the bed, the shutters still banging, wood against wood, in convulsive, sporadic blows. He took out the box of matches and struck one. The flame drew Andrushenko's eyes as it floated towards them. Still he said nothing.

Stenski's hand was absolutely steady. 'It may be necessary to hold him,' he said. 'Be prepared for that.' Johnson came vaguely forward, unsure of his role. The flame was only inches away now. Andrushenko must have felt the heat from it across his face. He snapped his head to one side and whispered a few words, almost inaudibly, as if he were ashamed of his own weakness.

Stenski stepped back, dropped the match and extinguished it with his foot; walked stiffly over to close the shutters. 'We will get him to write the letter in a few minutes. It would be a good idea to post it today.'

Stenski produced a pen and notepad from his suitcase. 'You will observe,' he remarked to Johnson, 'that this is Swedish paper. The watermark says as much. It is just the sort of paper Andrushenko would have bought here, if he had wished to write a letter.' Back in the bedroom, Stenski said: 'Untie him. Secure his feet to something. I must have his hands free.' Andrushenko sat up and wrung his wrists where the rope had bitten into them. Stenski handed him the notepad. 'I will dictate a letter to you. You will merely copy down the words. Please do not forget that I can read Russian as well as speak it.' Andrushenko looked up at him, uncomprehending. 'Then, when we have finished, you can have a bath. You are beginning to smell, if I may say so.'

Stenski must have rehearsed the letter enough, right down to the punctuation. He hardly hesitated.

Dear Sergei Markov!

I send you this letter because only you will understand it. I write it from Sweden, which is very cold, like our own country, in winter. I know that I cannot be found here, and that is why I am writing. You must already understand by my absence that I have made a very difficult decision. I will tell you the reasons later. I must assure you immediately that I have no intention of doing anything foolish. I offer my record of loyalty over twenty years as my guarantee. All I want is to live here, with a companion I have found. I want to be left alone. That will involve money. As you know, I was never well paid, certainly not well enough to support two people here, where everything, even the most trifling items, are more expensive than you can imagine. Twenty roubles for a kilo of butter!

Andrushenko wrote quickly, the nib of the pen scraping against the crisp paper. He did not even look at Stenski, who was standing over him, speaking clearly and precisely. He wrung his wrists again, but Stenski pressed him.

'Continue . . . '

I do not wish to speak here of the suffering I have undergone in making my decision. You and I, we have seen too much for stupid women's tears! I cannot speak, even, about the money, or about my future, and how it might affect you, unless we meet. I have reflected a long time about this and there seems no other alternative. I have no wish to take the knowledge I have gained elsewhere. I am tired now. I have devoted my life to our work. I only want to rest. I therefore propose a meeting. I know that this would not be difficult for you to arrange. You have the right of unquestioned travel, such a wonderful privilege! I will have it soon, when I am naturalised. Yes, Sergei Markov, I have decided even to do that.

Send a telegram to the central post office in Stockholm, marked for collection by Jan Olufsen. Please do not be so innocent as to imagine that I will go there myself, don't send anybody to meet me! I shall telephone to see if the telegram is there. The act of sending it will be sufficient confirmation. I propose that you come next Wednesday, the 21st. Come alone. Go to the central post office. It is in a street called Fleminggatan. A letter will be waiting for you, with a meeting place. Then we can have our little conversation. Please do not worry, Sergei Markov. We will discuss all questions as friends.

(Signed)
Alexis.

Stenski took the four pages of notepaper which the letter had covered and read each word with exaggerated care. He nodded in approval. 'Now the envelope. That is of the first importance.' He turned to Andrushenko. 'You understand that your future depends on this letter being safely delivered? To me, you have no importance. If this letter does not reach him, your position becomes very difficult.' He pressed the ends of his fingers together, summarising the situation. The marks on Andrushenko's wrists had risen like welts, as if the dry skin had been burned; a pattern of the lacerations crept back up his forearms, where the rope had slid upward. 'You will address this envelope simply: Sergei Markov,

Department of Security, Vilnius Street, Moscow. You will mark it strictly personal and confidential.' Stenski watched as Andrushenko wrote on the envelope. Stenski took the envelope when he had finished and inspected it with equal care. He folded the letter and placed it inside the envelope.

'The question was how best to transmit this letter,' Stenski said to Johnson. 'I thought at first that one might simply place it in the most convenient post box, but it would take a long time to reach Moscow, weeks perhaps. The Russians are very inefficient. Then I thought: They have constructed a system, those people. Why not use it?'

He turned back to Andrushenko, who was still holding the pen in his hand, not knowing if he would be required to do anything further.

'Another letter,' Stenski said, handing him the notepad again. 'Shorter, this time.' It was the faintest touch of humanity, but lost on the Russian. 'Begin.'

Dear Comrade Levnitch!

I entrust you with the enclosed letter to be delivered through diplomatic channels to the address on the envelope. The letter must on no account be opened. It should be forwarded as quickly as possible. Speed is essential.

I am working on an operation which I am not permitted to reveal to anyone!
(Signed)
A fellow-comrade.

'That is the end of the letter. Now the envelope. Write this: Anton Levnitch, Department of Protocol and International Relations, Embassy of the Union of Soviet Socialist Republics, Kungsgatan, Stockholm 3.' He turned to Johnson. 'The letter for Markov will be placed inside this one. The man Levitch will, of course, open the larger one addressed to him. He will certainly not dare to open the smaller one, marked for Moscow. He will merely forward it in the diplomatic bag. It will be there within three days. The only remaining question is: Should you deliver it to their Embassy in Kungsgatan, or put it in a post box? On this, I have not yet decided.'

'Post it here somewhere,' Johnson suggested. 'It will reach Stockholm in a few hours. The Swedes are supposed to be very hot like that.'

'Possibly so,' he reflected. 'Of course you will have to buy a stamp. That is one of the things I was not able to do before we came. They are not available in Vienna. That would mean waiting until morning, when the post offices are open again.' He began placing the smaller envelope inside the larger one. 'Such a shame Markov never ever came out of Russia himself. We could have taken him, and been spared all this.'

They went down to the lounge. Outside, the moon was ghostly behind the scudding clouds.

'McClellan said something very strange on the telephone this morning.' Johnson had been searching for the moment to bring it up. 'The Atkins case is closed. Barnard has apparently discovered nothing. At least that was the impression I got.

253

They have taken him off it.'

Stenski was not surprised. 'A most offensive man,' he said.

'But why haven't they put somebody else on it? Atkins was one of us, you can't just shut your eyes and pretend it never happened. It was murder, regardless of the implications for the intelligence service.'

'London always have their reasons,' Stenski said.

Johnson wondered what he would cook for supper. 'Do you really think Markov will come?'

Stenski sat in an arm chair. His body was limp, as if he were suddenly resting it. 'He has no alternative. None at all.'

⋆ ⋆ ⋆

Barnard stood at the end of Friedrichstrasse, facing the checkpoint, 200 yards away. Mid-morning. The snow had all melted now, leaving a drained, threadbare city, soulless and austere; a Prussian city and a sad city which had surrendered the reflection of what it had been, and was now camped out in the winter.

Only the Christmas trees in the shop windows offered warmth to the human condition. What does it amount to, Barnard wondered? A half of a city, rebuilt in a hurry and rebuilt in affluence: Block after block of apartments; underground shopping precincts, with unsmiling people transported up and down on metal escalators where the last of the leaves had gathered, and the wind was funnelled into the subterranean passages which they called arcades.

He looked again at the checkpoint and lit a cigarette. He was taking a risk. He hadn't contacted McClellan. He was backing himself to get back, and if he found out who killed Atkins, he would have stuffed them all.

He lumbered slowly forward along the pavement. It was eleven thirty. He had allowed himself an hour for formalities at the checkpoint, and that still gave him half an hour to spare. He reached the hut in the middle of the road at the intersection with Kochstrasse. The wall was thirty or forty yards away. Two West

Berlin customs men sat in the hut, talking casually. One of them looked at his passport but did not open it. He waved him through.

The Wall faced him now, ten feet high and made of breeze blocks cemented together. It stretched away in both directions along a wide channel where the houses had been cleared away.

Here, at exactly the width of Friedrich-strasse, was the checkpoint itself: A gap in the wall with a control tower right in the middle of it, painted white; a mushroom shape rising to an enclosed platform. He walked uneasily towards the first of the poles which lay, waist high, across the road. As he came, a soldier behind the platform glass moved imperceptibly, lifted binoculars and surveyed him. Stupid bastards, Barnard thought. The range was too short for binoculars to be any use. It was probably the regulations.

Two soldiers were stationed at each end of the pole. They stood immobile, hands locked behind their backs, sten guns on straps over their shoulders. They, too, were covered by the tower.

Barnard went right and the soldier challenged him.

'Purpose of visit to the DDR?' He wore a metal, shaped helmet, just like his father would have done. A different army, but . . .

'Tourism,' Barnard said.

'Proceed to the first hut.' The soldier stood back and allowed Barnard to go through the narrow passage between the end of the pole and the wall itself. The poles were just for vehicles.

Three nissen huts flanked the road; behind them, following the contours of the wall and invisible from the western side, were the other deterrents: The mined earthen strip, then the barbed wire. He went to the first hut. Four men and a girl sat at different counters, each in blue uniform. One of the men beckoned him over.

'Purpose of visit to the German Democratic Republic?'

'Tourism.'

'Passport?'

Clockwork people, Barnard thought. All programmed to say the same words.

The man turned each page of the passport with great care, then swivelled on his chair and thrust it through a square hole in the rear wall.

'You are obliged,' he said in stunted English, 'to buy a minimum of 100 DDR marks. You must do this in the next building. Then you will return here for your passport.'

Barnard went out and into the adjacent hut. It was laid out in exactly the same way, with a crude board giving the day's exchange rates against western currencies. He paid in West German marks, and the woman who served him opened a metal box full of notes and coins, and counted out 100. The notes were well handled. He counted them slowly. Play them at their own game, he thought.

His passport was waiting. It bore, on one of the inner pages, the visa stamp: a pale green compass wreathed in a circle of sheaves of wheat, designed to imitate the hammer and sickle.

The second pole lay before him now. Again two soldiers. He went right, was challenged.

'Passport?'

He handed it across. The soldier flicked the pages until he reached the visa, closed the passport and returned it; stood aside. Barnard was through.

His first impression, as he walked toward Leipzigerstrasse, was the strongest. Here it was, the missing half; here it was, the other winter, the longer winter, the spiritual winter. The buildings were of grey stone; there were gaps between them where the bombs had fallen, and the rubble still lay, thirty years on, with long grass pushing up through the piles of broken masonry. The houses which still stood had official slogans on them instead of advertising hoardings, and giant drawings of Lenin. The roads were empty of traffic and, at the corner of each street, groups of sullen pedestrians stood not moving and not talking.

So this is it, he reflected bitterly: The Promised Land.

The roads were not repaired. The coating of tarmac had worn away in places, down to the cobblestones underneath, and some of the cobblestones were

259

missing, too. In front of each cavity, red lamps had been placed to warn approaching drivers.

Barnard sensed people watching him. Perhaps it was his clothes, the cut of his coat. An old tram passed, heavy faces pressed against its windows. The queue for it was too long at Nuschke, and most were turned away. They milled about for a few moments like mute, discontented cattle then settled again to their wait. He reached Unter den Linden, and that was a little better. At least there were trees. He gazed down the broad avenue towards the Brandenburg Gate but the curvature of the road prevented a view of the Wall at its base.

The Happy Labourer was in the other direction, towards a wide square with a bombed out church at one side, its roof a web of exposed, rusting girders. He entered the beerhouse. It was one deep room which stretched back into the interior of the building, sawdust on the wooden floor; furnished with wooden tables and chairs, and a long bar. He sat at the table nearest the door. The daily papers were clipped to a stick, and the regulars passed them round. He checked the time: He had forty minutes to spare. A waiter appeared with a towel slung over his arm. Barnard ordered a beer.

He looked around. It was, he reflected, the wrong place to meet: Too public. He should have chosen somewhere else, but then he would have had no guarantee she would have come. Too late now.

She was punctual. She pushed the plate-glass door open carefully, as if she was afraid it might shatter; searched for him. He lifted an arm to signify recognition. She came over and sat.

She was medium height, with a pleasant, unremarkable face. She wore a black fur coat. She removed the matching fur hat and laid it on her lap. The hair was not as blonde as he had expected.

'Drink?' Barnard asked.

'Only a coffee.'

She looked almost coyly away from his glance.

'Can't we go somewhere more . . . private?'

'I don't think that would be a good idea,' she said.

'This place is worse than a railway station.' She shrugged. 'So let's do it here. I don't suppose it matters.'

'What have you come for?'

She wore too much lipstick and it had smeared her front teeth. The waiter arrived with the coffee on a tray: Two small pots, one coffee, the other warm water. The milk was in a tiny jug.

'What have you come for?' she repeated mechanically.

He lit a cigarette. Five stubbed ends were already in the ashtray, all his own. 'Listen, lady, a man got killed a while ago. A man you knew very well. His name was Atkins. All the evidence suggests that you were implicated. OK. I know where we are, I know we are in East Berlin and all you have to do is shout out to have me grabbed right here, but you had better listen good and hard because I haven't come over on a social visit.' He drew on the cigarette and she glanced at the nicotine on the first two fingers of his right hand.

'I hope you didn't tell anybody about

this meeting. Otherwise, you'd better never leave East Berlin again.'

'It's too late for all that,' she said. 'I'm not going anywhere.' She poured the coffee uncertainly. No sugar. 'You're a month too late.'

He didn't pursue it. He wanted to clear the ground first. She was nervous, and he knew it. 'Let's talk about Atkins. That is why I came. I want to know who killed him.'

'I couldn't kill anyone.' It was a simple, incontrovertible fact.

'Tell me about Atkins.'

She paused, considered her words. 'He was someone I worked with years ago. He was English or Canadian, I can't remember.' She gathered her composure back around her. 'That's all.' She might have practiced the phrase.

Barnard stooped until his face was close to her. 'Don't tell me lies,' he said between his teeth.

'What do you mean?' She feigned indignation.

'Stupid lies. Don't waste both our time.'

She fingered the hat, and he thought for a moment she was going to stand up and leave.

Barnard said: 'You worked with Atkins. That's nice and official and provable. End of story. Except you saw him after you left Holmstangl, and pretty regularly. Enough for him to have trailed you round, even to his golf club. I have the dates when you went there, in case you're interested.'

She closed her eyes.

''Look at this,' Atkins used to say. 'Look at the humming bird I've caught!' The boys were very impressed.'

'It is not an offence to see people,' she said. 'Not even here.' She lifted the cup of coffee, and put it down again without drinking. He hadn't touched the beer since her arrival. 'He was a happy sort of man and he liked company. I was alone. My husband . . . let's forget that.'

'I know all about your husband.'

'I am sure you are very thorough. But of course, between married couples there must be certain things which are not recorded and you cannot know.'

'Like that he used to beat you? Very Teutonic.'

'That and more. I do not wish to discuss it.'

'You couldn't even defend yourself. You're not physically strong enough. That's how I know you didn't kill Atkins. It would have taken a man to do that kind of job on him. They do say, incidentally, that they kept on beating him long after he was dead.'

She looked away, her eyes closed once more.

'Did you love him?' It was the instant for the question, and the instant might not come back.

'No,' she said, looking suddenly forlorn and abandoned. 'With a man like that, it cannot be love. At least, not in any sense which you would understand.' She did drink from the raised cup this time, and left a curve of lipstick at its rim.

'Why not tell me from the beginning?'

'I was a secretary at Holmstangl when he began work there. They employed him in the export department, because of his English, I suppose. Apart from his own work, he used to correct the grammar in the letters we wrote in English. He always carried a big ink pen, he hated biros, and he would underline the incorrect word and write the correct one in the margin. He did it so quietly, as if he was apologising to us for our own mistakes.'

'And?'

'He was not like a German. Of course. Excuse me, but the observation is not so amusing as you seem to feel. He worked hard but he did not draw his happiness from work alone. I had never met anyone before who had escaped from the work ethic. Do you find that so strange? You do not understand Germans. He had time for you, and he remembered small things which are important to a woman. He always wanted to know what you had bought when you had been out shopping. Once I came back with a fancy hat. When he came into my office, he insisted I try it on. He even went out and came back with a hand mirror, so that I could see myself. Then he just said: 'Beautiful'.'

She poured more coffee. Barnard's hand rested round the base of the beer glass like a paw. The foam had gone, and the liquid looked yellow and flat.

'Of course it was all very flattering. Women do not always ask themselves whether the compliments are sincere or not. On balance, we judge that they are.' She smiled for the first time. 'Some of the other girls thought he overdid it, but that is only because they did not understand him.' She lost herself for a moment, and she must have been thinking far, far back. 'Then I left Holmstangl. I found a better job as a personal assistant. We kept in touch, if you want to know the truth. He used to ring me up and say: 'Eva, the office is so empty without your smile.' He was so . . . harmless. I liked him and I liked his little moustache. Sometimes he would call me up and we would go out to dinner together.'

'What did your husband say to all that?'

'He never knew. Things were beginning to go wrong then. I think I would have gone anyway. At the end of the evening. Atkins would kiss me on the cheek and the taxi always took him home first so that we should not be seen together. He did not drive well, and the autobahns frightened him. 'Too fast for me, Eva,' he said.'

'You never mentioned him to your husband?'

'No.'

Barnard leant forward and gripped her arm. 'Congratulations. You should write books. Fictional books.' The waiter, standing away behind the counter, noticed the movement. Barnard withdrew the arm.

'It's the truth,' she said.

'Don't take me for a fool.'

He lifted the glass, retained it at an angle to his mouth and just let the beer flow into him, an oddly masculine gesture. 'When did you first sleep with Atkins?'

She hesitated in the ill-defined area between self-control and complete breakdown; she could have moved either way.

'If you must know, soon after he came to Holmstangl,' she said. 'Oh Christ, it's so long ago. Does it matter anymore, please?'

He nodded gravely, a priest at confession; the same seriousness, the same all-embracing comprehension; the same promise of forgiveness. 'Tell me.'

'He was not the kind of man you associate with . . . with physical sex. It was the way he looked at you. Like a dog with drooping, sad eyes. He lived alone, he was fifty, he didn't have much money, at least, not by German standards. I don't suppose he had had an affair for thirty years — that's what the great joke at Holmstangl used to be. Has he ever done it? The secretaries used to giggle and gossip about it. They nick-named him The Poodle. Just call, and he'll come running to have his back rubbed. I'm sure he knew. He was so sensitive. The men were just as cruel. Men can be worse sometimes. He never once said anything against them, not even when we had become intimate . . . when it would have been safe for him to do so. They had an office football team at Holmstangl, they played on a pitch just behind the factory.'

'I know it.'

'They always asked him if he was frightened to play for them. 'The English,' they would say, 'invented all these sports, and you won't even play for our little team.' But he was fifty! They all knew that. He would go and stand on the touchline and cheer for them, by himself. Nobody else ever bothered to go and watch. When the game was over, they ignored him and he just came back to the office. If the team had won, he was always pleased.'

'But you did sleep with him.'

'It began one day when everybody else except me was out to lunch. I was crying. If you want to know, it was after something which happened between my husband and myself.'

'Like he beat you up.'

'Yes. Atkins came in just then and saw me. He put his arm round me and comforted me. He was very good at that. He radiated reassurance. You wouldn't understand. You cannot imagine how gentle he could be, like a cat. He had the hands of a doctor, warm and healing. He asked me to tell him everything, but only if I wanted to. I said I had left home because of my husband. Do you know what it is like when a drunken man comes back looking for any pretext for violence? There is no escape. He will find one. The food is too hot, the food is too cold. The dress you are wearing is too gay, too sad. Why have you not cleaned the carpets? Atkins offered to let me stay with him until things had sorted themselves out. What an exquisite English statement, and he translated it word for word so nothing was lost. I remember that phrase so well. He said I could have the bed and he would sleep on the settee. I know it sounds stupid, but I trusted him. He had never, as you would say, undressed me with his eyes. But of course my husband rang back in the afternoon and apologised, so I went home instead.'

Gently does it, Barnard told himself. Listen to the confession all the way to the end. She needs to confess. She couldn't have told all this to anybody else, not even the East Germans. It's virgin territory . . .

'It all happened a few weeks later. My husband came back drunk again one night. He could be evil. I refused to prepare him a meal. It was two in the morning. I said to him: 'What do you take me for, a galley slave? I have to work, too. I have a regular job. I have to sleep.' He struck me several times with his closed fist, even in the stomach. I thought I was going to die.

'I must have lain on the kitchen floor for a long time. It was half past four when I woke. My husband was asleep in bed. He made some dreadful noises when he slept. I remember hoping he would choke. I put my coat on and took a taxi.

'I gave the taxi driver Atkins' address. I had nowhere else to go at that time of the morning. I rang the bell. He appeared in a silk dressing gown — purple, I remember — looking more asleep than awake. He made me some cocoa. He didn't have anything to eat except chocolate biscuits. He was terribly upset by that. He found some blankets in a wardrobe and made up a bed on the settee. We argued about that. I told him it was stupid to give up his bed to a stranger at that hour. 'But you're not a stranger,' he said over and over again. He was emphatic. He could be very firm about things like that. I wore only a nightdress and overcoat. He left the room while I took the coat off and got into the bed. Then he wanted to change the sheets. He remembered that he had been sleeping in the bed. This time, I forbade him. I told him I was too tired. He accepted that, so he turned the light off. I couldn't sleep. I kept thinking every sound was my husband at the front door. He would have killed him. Atkins must have heard me restless because he came to me in the darkness and began to stroke my hair. He didn't say anything. But I wanted him. I could sense his breathing close to me. I wanted him to be a father and a lover. I wanted his strength. I suppose that was unfortunate. He wasn't that kind. When he stroked my hair, it was like a child stroking a bird with a broken wing. I told him I wanted him. He was very embarrassed. He said he had no contraceptives. I could have laughed. Where had

273

he been all those years? I told him they were not necessary. He was not very good at making love. When it was over, I thought he was going to cry. He switched the light on and sat at the end of the bed, by himself. 'Look at me,' he said. 'A girl comes to me in trouble, her eyes heavy with tears, and this is what I do to her. This!' In spite of that, I thought he had taken a certain pleasure from the act of love. Perhaps I am too cynical.'

She drank more coffee.

''Forgive me,' he said. 'It has been so long since anything like this happened. I thought I had learned to control it. I don't even look at dirty magazines any more!' I had to coax him back into the bed. He kissed me on the ear, and we both went to sleep.

'Later, I went home. I told my husband that I had spent the night with a girlfriend. He accepted that. After his behaviour, he had no choice.'

'And you kept on seeing Atkins?'

'Most weeks, only once. He was like a habit I acquired. He never varied. Sometimes we would go to the golf club.

Sometimes we would go back to his apartment in the lunch hour and just sit talking. We didn't always make love. He was ashamed of his body and did not like it being seen in the daylight.'

'You also went there at night?'

'If I had a proper excuse. I told my husband that I used to go to netball training, to keep fit.'

'How long did this go on?'

'Until Atkins was killed.' She began to sob softly, took a tiny handkerchief out of her handbag and dabbed at her eyes, prudently and unobtrusively, so that nobody would notice. 'He wanted to marry me. He said he could get a job in England, though not for so much money. He said I wouldn't have to work any more. He said he would buy a little house in a village, out in the country. Then he'd stop and say he was too old.

''I'm fifty six now.' He would do the equation. 'You are thirty one. When I'm sixty six, you'll be forty one: such a lovely age, forty one, experience and beauty both coming together. Seventy six, fifty one.' He would whisper that with a terrible finality. 'You'll spend all the best years of your life caring for an invalid — and in a foreign country!''

Her sobbing was like water being drawn from a deep, almost barren well. 'If only everything had been different,' she said. Barnard's cigarette had burned into a horn of ash close to the fingers which held it like a pincer. It was extinguished itself, and he let it fall into the ashtray; clicked the same two fingers for another beer.

'He didn't even make love very well,' she said at last. 'Sometimes he failed altogether. At first, that was embarrassing. A woman can feign that, you know, but a man can't. But in an odd way, it brought us closer. He would say: 'If you like me in spite of that, the bond between us is very strong.''

Her eyes were veined in red after the crying, the hoods half down.

The beer came.

Barnard said: 'Did you know that he had another job while he was at Holmstangl?'

'Not at first. I can't even remember

how it came out. It was an awful shock. Him, of all people.'

'How much did he tell you?'

'Enough. I didn't want details.'

'Names, things like that? Did he ever let you see correspondence, telephone numbers? Ever tell you who he was meeting and where and what time?'

'No.'

Christ, Barnard thought, Christ, she must have known. A secretary, a German secretary, half-crazy about him, had access to all that little lot. He took a mouthful of the new beer, and the froth lingered on his lips. He wiped it crudely away with the back of his hand.

'Did you ever help him in his work — even indirectly?'

'No.' She looked straight at him. 'He cared for me too much to involve me.'

'Very touching.' There was a chill in Barnard's voice now, a hardening of his purpose. 'Come on dear, you were with him half the time, you couldn't have avoided it — run a few errands, answer the telephone, help with the clerical work — you know, type letters.'

'I have already told you: No.'

Her half-finished coffee had turned cold. A film of dark brown skin was forming across it like scum.

'So you worked for the East Germans instead? Sorry to put it so bluntly.' In turn he looked at her: No games now.

'I am not prepared to talk about that,' she said with total conviction. 'I have been very honest so far, mainly because we have something in common: We both want to know who killed him. You for your reasons, me for mine. But you can't make me talk about that.'

He paused. 'Did you see him that night?'

She nodded, adjusted her hands on her lap, a nervous gesture. 'Every night he walked the caretaker's dog across the playing field. He always went the same way round, and never strayed onto the pitches, even in the darkness when nobody would have been able to see him. He was very correct. He would have liked a dog of his own, but they were forbidden to tenants. And of course he had to go to work all day.'

'It happened on a Monday . . . '
Barnard hesitated, wondering how she
would take it, how long she'd keep
talking. 'Tell me in detail please.' It was a
civil request, and he made damn sure it
sounded civil to her, too.

'You mean, did we make love? I
thought you would ask that. No, as a
matter of fact, we did not. I met him at
his apartment. I went on the U bahn, and
walked the rest of the way. He couldn't
cook, really. He would fill the kitchen
with smoke and have to open all the
windows. He would come into the lounge
with an apron round his waist and say: 'I
am so sorry, but it's all gone wrong
again!' He blamed the recipe books. That
was one of our jokes. But he never
permitted me to cook at the apartment.
'No, my dear, you have a full-time job,
and a husband to look after. You can't
manage two husbands. You must rest
when you are here, and I will be your very
own servant.' '

'Why are you laughing?'

'Never mind.'

The rain was heavier. It must have been

nearly half past three, and the street lights would be on soon.

'I left at about nine o'clock. I had to get home to my husband. You can check the timings with him if you don't believe me. I am happy to give you his present address, unless he has moved since I last saw him. But I am sure a man like you would find him, in any case.' She gazed at the coffee, useless and undrinkable. 'He said he was going to walk the dog when I left. He kissed me on the forehead. The television was on — so people couldn't hear us talking — and the evening news bulletin had just begun. It must have been almost exactly nine. He stood at the door until I had gone down the stairs. That was the last time I saw him.'

He thought she was going to cry again. 'What I want to know,' he said quickly, 'is who killed him. Let me clarify that. I am not particularly interested in who actually did it. I met your friend the other day, the one who hangs around with Klaus. They could have done it, you know. You couldn't prove to me they didn't. But I left them. I want the person who gave the order. You see the difference? Any stupid thug could have broken Atkins' head open, any passing bus driver, any policeman, any football player. I'm looking for the person who wanted him killed. And if his memory is so sacred to you, I think you had better tell me.'

The rain was slanted against the window pane, dribbling down it in rivulets.

'I will tell you only this: The East Germans were very surprised when it happened. I received a message instructing me to cross the border immediately. They told me to leave everything in West Berlin and just drive across regardless.'

'Why?'

'I don't know.'

'Because they didn't want you picked up on the western side and made to talk?'

'I suppose so. If the order had been given here, why would the East Germans not have brought me over the day before?'

'Maybe they felt that would alert Atkins?'

She shrugged. 'They were surprised when it happened. I could tell: I didn't have time to pack.'

She looked at her watch. The rush hour was just beginning, more pedestrians than cars. 'I must go now,' she said decisively.

'I want to talk about a lot of other things,' Barnard said. 'We've only just begun.'

'I am sorry.' She arranged the fur hat fastidiously towards the back of her head while he went to the counter and paid. He didn't know whether to tip or not, decided against, and held the door open while she stepped out onto the pavement. He turned his collar up against the rain.

They took a few paces side by side, going back in the direction of the distant Brandenburg Gate. Two Muscovite cars were parked at the kerb twenty yards ahead, but the rain on their windows prevented him seeing if anybody was inside. When they drew level with the first car, the doors both opened and, from behind him, Barnard heard a voice he knew.

'Mr. Barnard, please get into the first car. This one, not that one.'

He turned and was looking at Gause.

Eva was already moving away. 'I'm sorry,' she said. 'I had to tell them.'

Now — at that precise moment, which would extend itself to a few seconds but not more — now was the time to move. They were off balance, in the rain, spread: Gause behind, two men advancing from the cars in front. But there was nowhere to run; he might get away, into the rush-hour crowd struggling home, might lie low, if he was lucky, for a couple of days on a bomb site, but he would never get back, across the barbed wire and the minefields and the Wall. Never.

The moment was gone. He was still standing, erect and unmoving. He couldn't even pretend he had a gun. They wouldn't care, not three of them.

Pedestrians backed away, took a detour round the group. Don't ask questions, don't get involved, that was the creed. He couldn't even call out for help.

'All right,' he said, not turning round. 'But tell your bully boys that if one of them lays a finger on me, I'll hurt him.'

'The first car,' Gause said. It was an

order, not an invitation. 'As for what the men do: I will decide that.'

★   ★   ★

The lake absorbed Stenski. He watched it more and more, and that suited Johnson because it was at those hours spent near the kitchen window, contemplating the ice and the water, that Stenski would communicate; or, at least, could be drawn into communication.

'Do you really believe Markov will come?' Johnson asked. He had posted the letter and they had settled back into the waiting. 'What about all that intuition you talk about so much? He'll smell this all the way from Moscow.'

'I am inclined to agree,' Stenski said, 'that he will be understandably suspicious, though the fact that the letter comes to him from Sweden and not Austria will give it enormous authenticity. He is being offered a proposition. He cannot prove that the letter is anything but genuine until he meets Andrushenko. In the meantime, he may suspect what he wishes. That will not allay the pressure on him domestically. Here is Andrushenko, a senior man, a man trusted to go abroad, who defects ostensibly to live with a woman — that, of course, is the interpretation they will place upon the word 'companion' in the letter. They must interpret it like that when they consider Andrushenko's case-history, his disgrace in Berlin. That will all be in his file, and they will turn it up.' When he spoke, his eyes never left the lake and the hillside beyond. 'Here is Andrushenko, who could probably wreck half a dozen networks because of what he knows. A defection on that scale would certainly cost Markov his job. Let us consider what this involves. We know that he has a country house in that village where they all live . . . '

'Nikolina Gora?'

'Yes, that place. He would lose that. He would lose access to the special shops, the Beryozka shops, his chauffeur would go, his big Zil car would go; he would be denied a bed in the good hospitals. And he could never work his way back. It would be a catastrophe of the first magnitude.'

Stenski unlocked his hands and placed them with great care in his jacket pockets. 'They are not benevolent in their attitudes. They give access to luxury, and they take it away. He knows that better than we. That is why he will come: Because he has to.'

Andrushenko was sitting on the kitchen chair, his hands free. He looked very humble, like a prisoner of war; no rights, and his future to be decided by others. Stenski told him to stand up. He did so uncertainly; three days on the bed has wasted the muscles in his legs. 'Paul. Run the bath for him, please.'

Johnson said: 'Even if Markov does come he'll hardly come alone. What are we going to do if ten men show up?'

'Use a sieve. Shake it carefully enough and all the pebbles fall through: But the precious stone remains.'

After the bath, Andrushenko was permitted to walk about the house for an hour. 'Exercise him, Paul,' Stenski had said, 'but stay with him. Don't let him get hold of anything.'

'What happens to him afterwards? It's a bit late to think of that now.'

'Perhaps.' The implication was obvious: Stenski had already thought about it.

'I would like you to explain that.' Johnson was insistent now.

'Nothing.' Andrushenko sat on the kitchen chair again, looking exhausted. He stared vacantly at the wall in front of him. 'We could send him away, once the telegram comes.'

That was what angered Johnson. He understood Stenski, knew how he planned each move right to the end of the game; always had done. He knew how, constantly and maddeningly, Stenski told him just enough to keep him quiet.

'Send him where, for God's sake? You can't just release him.'

'Send him away, that's all. Somewhere safe, until it's over.'

'He would have to be accompanied. Which of us goes with him?'

'Neither.'

'Let's talk about this. I'm pretty pliable, some would say far too pliable. When I first came to Berlin, McClellan said: Watch Stenski, absorb his techniques, learn from him. Don't be subservient, we never require that, but regard yourself as a pupil.'

'That was the understanding.'

'And I honoured it.'

Stenski nodded. He had no vanity, and had become an elder statesman quite unconsciously.

'That was two years ago. We are not equals. Of course. But I have rights, unlike him.' He motioned toward Andrushenko, who sensed that he was being discussed and looked up, uncomprehending. 'I have rights because I share the risks. Sometimes the risks are all mine, remember?' There would always be friction between them; with Stenski that was inevitable. Both men were conscious of it and lived with it.

'I want to know what happens to Andrushenko.' The Russian recognised his name again and shook his head. He had sunk back into his position in life. The other kind of obedience, more comprehensive, reaching further. 'What becomes of him?' Johnson needed the emphasis of repetition.

'He stays. That seems to be the best way, since you are so concerned. I have some more serum in my suitcase, and a supply of needles. The doctor gave them to me. We will put him to sleep again when we need to — tie him up again now.'

'That's inhuman. Look at him — he hasn't the strength to stand up properly. You may be a masochist, but I'm not. We've already nearly torn his wrists to pieces. He can hardly move about. And you want to tie him up again.'

'You talk like the people in London,' Stenski said. He was not in the least agitated because he understood the English character perfectly well, and he knew that Johnson would come to heel. 'I have told you, as I told them: If you want to run a service like this, you have to do these things. Get a little mud on your hands. And don't you forget, they weren't so delicate with Atkins.'

It was the first time, the very first time, he had mentioned the name.

'Andrushenko didn't kill Atkins. He was working in another sector, minding his own business, trying to screw a woman when we took him. I accept that he may not be a particularly savory character. But we owe him a little dignity. Let him wander round the house for a while. Let him wash by himself, let him clean his teeth without supervision. Go to the bloody toilet without an escort. Let him close the toilet door if he wishes. I don't want to stand there on the landing watching him do it any more. That's all.'

'In that case, I will watch him. In the camps, they had communal toilets, everybody together. It does not trouble me.'

'You want to hurt him and that's the real truth. You don't forgive. It's a corporate guilt, and you want to punish them all, even the innocent bystanders.'

'This man — who moves you to pity so easily — has never, so far as one can tell, shown any human being any measure of pity. He probably would not even comprehend the word. He raped East German girls when he had only to crook his finger and they belonged to him. I will tell you something about the method he employed then: He allowed them to get out of his car, then when he had wound the window down he instructed them to lean in to embrace him as a way of saying goodnight. When their heads came through the window he would wind it up, trapping them by the neck. Then, when they were helpless there, he did what he wished. What about their dignity?'

Johnson went to the lounge and took up the rope from the table, where he had laid it.

\*   \*   \*

Barnard sat in the back of the car, next to Gause. The driver, who wore a leather raincoat and reminded Barnard of an American gangster between the wars, was hunched uncomfortably over the wheel. The other car followed at a respectable distance. They travelled along the Linden and turned right. The driver did not need instructions. He manipulated the car with exaggerated care, stopping at all the traffic lights when they were red. The interior of the car was as sombre as the darkness which had fallen; almost a hearse. In the suburbs, they passed a column of military vehicles. That was all Barnard would remember of the journey, that and the endless streets of partially restored tenement buildings and the unexpected clearings, with workers' apartments rising from them, each apartment containing a narrow, cramped balcony too small for sunbathing.

'I am surprised you came,' Gause said. He wore the same clothes as when he had met Barnard before: Only the briefcase was absent. 'It was hardly a shrewd thing to do, professionally speaking. I knew you were headstrong, but . . . ' He relapsed into silence. They were moving past parkland, down an avenue of trees illuminated by the street lamps which picked out the pools of rainwater on the road. 'The Voroshilov leisure centre,' Gause observed, 'to your left. In summer, it is a great favourite with the children. During August, a big travelling fair is organised. It is very pleasant. By the way, don't be too hard on the woman Eva.' The park had gone now and they were back among the houses. 'She is not exactly a convert. She was only doing what she was told.'

'What the hell does that mean?'

'Meaning when you had your accident. And today.' He lifted his left arm and pointed towards Barnard's cheek, then smiled, a grim, satisfied smile.

At a crossroads, a small car pulled out across them and the driver had to brake hard. He uttered a curse as the small car went away down a side road.

'A Russian,' Gause said. 'They do not observe the priority on the main highways. Nobody knows why.'

Barnard saw the white sign soon after, nailed to staves on the grass verge on both sides of the road: Ministry of Internal Security of the German Democratic Republic: No admittance to unauthorised personnel.

The building lay some distance away at the rear of the bombsite. It was enclosed in a compound of wire mesh. A soldier came forward out of the shadows and challenged them, his breath visible as it condensed in the chilled air. Gause opened his window, spoke a single word and the soldier went back down the road, into the margins of light from a beam on a tower playing across the road. His boots clattered on the tarmac.

The twin mesh gates were pulled back and the car moved cautiously through. The escorting car described a laboured three-point turning thirty yards from the gates and went away.

They drove slowly into a courtyard, and the red-brick building was all around them, like a barracks. Searchlights flooded down onto the cobblestones of the square. Barnard looked around. The windows were all boarded over. A door opened and Gause indicated for him to go through. As the door closed behind him, he heard the car moving away. He wouldn't be going home tonight.

The corridor had been painted cream, a charmless, utility cream, as cheap as distemper. They walked far down it, past half a dozen closed wooden doors, each unmarked, and their footsteps echoed on the stone slabbed floor; they went down a stone staircase to a lower level and a similar corridor. It was dimly lit. The doors here were metal and studded. One was ajar, the light on within.

It was a plain cell. The walls were brick, and painted over with the same cream. The central light was encased in a mesh basket so that it could not be touched. To its left, a fresh air fan turned noiselessly, also behind mesh. The furniture was bleak: A low iron bed with a mattress and a single grey blanket, folded in a square, at the foot of it; a table in the centre, with a chair at either side, facing each other.

'Sit over there,' Gause said. He indicated the chair at the far side.

Barnard sat. He was almost too big for the chair.

Gause left without saying anything or closing the metal door behind him. He came back after a few minutes with a man in uniform, who surveyed Barnard briefly, offered no comment, drew back the other chair and sat down.

'This is Colonel Karman of the People's Security. He is very interested in you.' Gause had pulled the door closed and leant against the wall next to it. 'Colonel Karman speaks excellent English — apart from his other accomplishments.'

Barnard looked at Karman, no more than three feet away: A tall, proper man with the classic Teutonic features, fair hair and blue eyes.

'How charming,' Barnard observed. 'All we need is a vicar and we can have a tea party. Your English good enough to get that?' He looked at Karman, but whether he understood or not Barnard couldn't tell. Karman was holding himself stiff, a parade ground posture he retained even when seated. He had not removed the field green flatpeeked cap, encircled by a strand of gold braid.

'What am I supposed to do now: Give my name, rank and serial number, then tell you to go to hell?' Barnard said. He pushed his chair backwards so that he had more leg room, and looked directly at Karman. 'And where did they produce you from, sonny?'

'A little bravado,' Gause commented from far away. 'Exactly what one would anticipate at the beginning, from someone with your personality.' He moved away from the wall and drifted a little closer, hands in his trouser pockets. 'But remember, you are not in London now, not even in West Berlin. If you want to make things more difficult for yourself . . . ' He smiled, a sickly, milk-and-water smile. 'Colonel Karman has a very big reputation . . . '

'I bet he has,' Barnard said. 'I just bet he has. He looks a pretty big man to me, safe behind the barbed wire in a brick cell. Does he talk, too?'

'You can smoke,' Gause said, noting Barnard reaching into his pocket.

'What is this — an old pal's reunion?'

'Mr. Barnard,' Karman said — and the voice was as cold as his eyes, as cold as the brick of the walls — 'You are a courageous man. Of this there can be no doubt. A coward would not have come to East Berlin. Now please stop behaving like a fool.'

Barnard measured him across the

table. The fan hummed evenly. Some-where, down the wall to the left and near the floor, someone had etched a slogan, probably with a piece of cutlery; An inmate's grafitti. Karman watched him, too. 'Gause,' he said, 'go away.' Gause pushed the door open and closed it noiselessly behind him.

'You may be tried,' Karman continued. 'You have committed several offences, and you could certainly expect a long term of imprisonment. Entry to the Democratic Republic under false pretences, threatening a citi-zen . . .'

Barnard chose not to reply.

'I think it would be better if we spoke frankly. I will ask you some questions. Your attitude will be judged by your answers.'

Barnard lit a cigarette and searched in vain for an ashtray.

'Throw the match on the floor. And the cigarette, when you have finished it. The rooms are cleaned out daily.'

'Almost a hotel,' Barnard said. 'I'm very impressed.' Karman did not catch the sarcasm; his English wasn't that good at all.

'When did you join British Intelligence?'

'The date?'

'Of course the date. Why did you think I asked this question if I did not wish to know the date?'

'1965 Autumn. I forget whether it was a Monday or a Tuesday.'

'And before that?'

'Army. Normal military service. Trained in England — a place called Pirbright — a year with the Army of the Rhine, a tour of Cyprus — sorted out a few wogs — back to the Rhine.'

'Please continue.'

'That was when I was recruited. I was seconded when I got back to Germany after Cyprus. Special duties. They must have thought I was promising material.'

'I want full details of your recruitment.'

'I've told you.'

'You have told me nothing.' The pitch of his voice sharpened. It was the first test. 'I want names, places, dates. Something . . . something concrete.'

'Get lost.'

'Everybody breaks, even the strong ones,' Karman said. 'I do not wish to sound dramatic. It is only a statement. Why not make it easy for yourself?'

'Get lost.'

Karman stood up, went to the door and knocked on it once. Gause came in 'Reason with him,' Karman said. 'I give you ten minutes.' Then he walked away, and Barnard could hear the regular sound of his footsteps fading down the corridor.

'Listen,' Gause began, 'you're crazy. Everybody starts off like you. They think they can bargain their way out, or bluff their way out, or beg their way out. It is not possible. They will keep on and on. They've got everything here, drugs, electric machines . . . ' He came to the rim of the table. There was a terrible intensity in his eyes and, for just a moment, Barnard thought it might have been genuine concern. 'Human life is not sacred here,' he whispered. 'Think about that. What do you imagine will happen if anybody asks questions in the west? The East German news agency will put out a paragraph saying that an English tourist is missing. Enquiries are going on. That will be the official line. They will keep on repeating that until nobody cares any more. And that won't be long.' Barnard dropped the cigarette and ground it into the stone floor with the heel of his shoe. 'So answer their questions, and then you can go.'

'I don't believe that for a start.'

'Why not?'

'Why the hell do you think?'

Barnard lit another cigarette, and counted how many remained in the packet: Seven. It wouldn't be enough to see him through. He'd have to think about rationing them, after he'd lit this one.

'If you are inhibited by certain things,' Gause said, moving back towards the wall, 'we didn't kill Atkins. Why should we?'

'Because you killed all the others. Jungermann . . .'

'We heard about that. Jungermann's death was a real automobile accident. Mr. Barnard, you have experience of these

301

things. Is an automobile accident not the most dangerous way of attempting to kill someone? I put that to you. They might survive, your own man might become involved in the crash . . . '

'You broke up the whole network. Atkins was the last.'

'Us? It was a Russian operation. You know that already, I imagine. Let us say it was a joint operation: The USSR and the Democratic Republic. The accent was Russian.'

'Yes, and you got through the whole bloody list, right down to Atkins.'

'Not Atkins.'

'Tell that to the fairies.'

'I do not understand.'

'Never mind.' He drew deep on the cigarette. 'Why not Atkins?'

'Because we had turned him. That was not so difficult. He was working for us.'

'Atkins was more English than Westminster Abbey. You couldn't turn a man like that.'

'They are the dangerous kind. On that, I am sure we will agree. Always observe the quiet ones most closely.'

'You seem pretty anxious to tell me all about it.'

'Why not? It can hardly be good for morale on your side. And Atkins is dead. He can harm nobody any more.'

'Who killed him? It was you, or Karman, or somebody on this side. Probably a Russian. The accent of the operation was Russian. You said that. But you personally turned him, he was your catch, your rotten stinking little contribution. You knew him, you came over nearly every week with your bag full of chemicals. You were like woodworm: Eating your way in. You set up the woman Eva. What was the bait for her? Money? Security? She thought she had found it with Atkins. Then you went for him. What was his bait? Tell me, I just can't imagine.'

Gause said: 'He was very English, terribly so. One had to be delicate to avoid hurting his sensibilities. You know that he loved the woman Eva?'

Barnard nodded. 'What turned him?' It came deep from his throat, like a cry for pity — not a request for information at all.

'Underneath, he was a deceitful bastard,' Gause said. Gause rapped on the door, and told a uniformed soldier to go and fetch Karman. 'He felt rejected. Poor little English Atkins wanted revenge on his own country. Why do you think he worked in Germany? He was dismissed by a firm in Birmingham — redundancy, they termed it. He was left with nothing but a miserable English pension. Rache — excuse me if I employ the German word. It is so much more expressive. Revenge: He wanted that like an ache in the stomach, against all of them, the people who had milked him and rejected him through all his working life. I discovered that very quickly. After that, it was only a question of strategy.'

'Did Atkins kill any of the other people in the network?'

'Hardly, although he was surprisingly competent. Really, I do not think you should know more.'

Karman returned and resumed his position on the chair.

Gause motioned with his hand. 'Reason has prevailed,' he said. 'Shall I leave you?'

'Stay.' Karman: Aged perhaps 40. He wouldn't even remember the War, Barnard reflected. He's a child of the propaganda, he's never known anything else. 'Let us recommence. Who recruited you?'

'Get lost.'

Karman turned to Gause, who shook his head as if he couldn't imagine how this had happened.

Barnard stood up, leaned forward and placed both his hands on the surface of the table. 'I can't tell you a damn thing,' he said. He heard the fan, monotone, but he saw only Karman's impassive eyes. 'What do you want anyway? To go back through a whole load of case-histories involving people you'd never even heard of?'

'I will be the judge of that.'

'Stupid bloody German,' Barnard sat down again and threw the cigarette away.

When Karman and Gause had gone, and the door had been bolted heavily on the outside, he took out the packet and counted them again: Six, after the one he'd just put in his mouth.

★　★　★

Johnson made the telephone call after three days. It was a prudent and respectable interval. Stenski was unhurried now, as if he had begun a process which would reach some conclusion whether he did anything or not; Johnson was merely bored. He wished for something to lose himself in, television, radio, books, newspapers, anything; but he had nothing. In the mornings, he walked to the lakeside alone, through a plantation of half-grown pine trees and stood looking out across the water. Occasionally he prised smooth stones from the frozen ground and cast them out across the level ice as far as he could, making them skim. He discovered an inlet with an abandoned rowing boat held in the ice flow, its side partially crushed as the ice had expanded. That was the only sign human beings had even been there.

On the third morning, Stenski said: 'Go and telephone now. Go to that village, it seemed far enough away.'

Johnson drove off a few minutes later, anxious to get away, see some shops, have a change . . . anything but Stenski and the man tied on the bed, who never spoke and had to be constantly watched.

Johnson walked casually to the post office, savouring the luxury of having normal people around him, busying themselves with everyday chores. It was a different woman behind the grille. Stenski had written the number on a piece of paper, and Johnson pushed it through.

'Cabin one,' the woman said as she began to dial.

He waited inside the cabin. The telephone rang after a few moments.

'Do you speak English?' Johnson asked.

'Yes.' It was a man at the other end.

'My name is Jan Olufsen,' Johnson said. 'I am Norwegian.' The telephone line would conceal his accent. 'I am on a business visit, and I told anybody who wanted to get in touch with me to do so through the central post office in Stockholm.'

'This is the central post office.'

'I am far from Stockholm. I wonder if you can inform me if there is any mail for me.'

'Please wait a moment.'

The cabin stank of something unpleasant. Three telephone directories hung from a rack, and people had scribbled numbers on their covers.

The man came back. 'One piece of mail.'

'What is it, please?'

'A telegram. It arrived last night. The time is stamped at 4.53.'

'Thank you. I shall have to try to come and collect it.'

When he came out of the post office, the sun was dipping over the rooftops. The ice had retreated from the pavements, leaving the scattered black grains of gravel which had been spread to give a foothold.

Well damn me, he thought. It's worked.

★ ★ ★

Barnard lay on the bed for an hour after pulling the blanket roughly across himself. He tried to sleep, but that was useless. The light was still on, there was no switch in the room. He hammered on the door and shouted: 'Toilet!'

They passed a tin can through the door and he used that; placed it, with a very proper regard for hygiene, in a corner of the cell, and lay down again.

When he woke, Gause was leaning against the wall, smoking his pipe. The smell must have woken him. 'I have been granted one last chance to talk to you,' Gause said. 'After that, I can do nothing more.' He held the pipe in one hand, nursing the bowl. 'It will be unpleasant. I am very happy it is not me.'

'Get lost.'

'What motivates you: Duty, pride, insensibility? They'll find out.' Gause shook his head in despair. 'It could have been so easy for both of us ... an exchange of information. You could have been back in West Berlin now, safe in that little office in the British Embassy. Instead of this.'

And Gause went out.

They came an hour later, three of them in white surgical tunics, forearms bare. Big men, Barnard noted. They made him stand up and pushed him out into the corridor.

'Forward,' one of them said in German.

They turned left at the end of the corridor, down steps and into another corridor, narrower. The door at the end was already open. It was a big room with all the apparatus of an operating theatre: A bed covered in white rubber sheeting, waist high so that those conducting an operation would not have to stoop; arc lamps on stands; machines on castors grouped nearby. Beyond them, the shadows. A tall man stood half in them filling a syringe. Barnard felt hands seize him from behind, forcibly undress him. He could smell surgical spirit thick in his nostrils. He was still struggling hard when they finished stripping him. Three men were too many. They forced him onto the bed on his back. Leather bands were passed round his wrists and ankles, and secured to rings at each corner of the bed. He was spreadeagled, looking directly into an arclamp above. It hurt his eyes and he closed them.

The doctor came across, holding the needle in his right hand. With the left he gripped Barnard's wrist in slender fingers, digging the thumb in to verify his pulse; hoisted the needle to the height of his own eye, examined it and pressed it into Barnard's arm. Barnard closed his eyes again and felt pain at the point where the needle had pierced him, seeping outward.

'Hey,' Barnard called out, 'where's the fearless Colonel Karman?'

'I am here.'

'Still got your cap on?' He laughed. The pain was getting worse. 'That's very impolite, you know, wearing it indoors. No breeding, that's your trouble.' He heard Karman's footsteps, tried to open eyes, and was unable to do it. He sensed Karman setting down a chair and adjusting it at the bedside.

'Let us recommence. Who recruited you?'

'Get lost.'

Karman waited; let the pain seep a little further. After that, Barnard heard only Karman's voice, close to him, a clipped, precise German voice, the one constant in the shifting patterns of darkness which had come over him. It bore no height and no depth, no evaluation of the importance of one question balanced against another; it went on and on, as a cutting saw continues, thin, scraping and jarring, devouring whatever is put before it.

Barnard felt he was being pressed downward and the room was turning with him held captive in the centre, down and down and down. He wanted to be physically sick, but his stomach seemed far away and detached, like a severed limb.

Only the voice did not change. Karman, clinical and uncaring, was working towards what he wanted.

'Names, dates, places.' There was a cadence to the sentence; by repetition, it had become a tribal chant. Barnard's head was hopelessly heavy, and he struggled to lift it from the flat bed.

'Names, dates, places.'

Barnard's lips were dry. The cavern of his mouth was as arid and sharp as sandpaper. The words were as detached as his stomach; his dry tongue seemed to

312

be coated in scales, and he could hardly formulate the phrases. But he knew what he was saying. He could hear his own voice, like an echo along a tunnel; but he drew comfort from that. They could compel you to talk, but they couldn't stop you knowing what you had said. He wondered savagely if he would remember.

'Names, dates, places.'

'What was your name?' Barnard asked. 'I seem to have forgotten.'

Karman let that go. 'Who recruited you? I want the name of the man.'

'Can't recall.' His lips parted. 'Wouldn't tell a bastard like you, anyway.'

Silence. Somebody moved their feet. Probably the doctor.

'When were you recruited?'

'In 1965. Autumn. I forget the day.' He raised his voice. 'I told you that already. Your memory is as bad as mine.'

Silence.

'Give him some more,' Karman said.

The doctor replied: 'Only a little.'

Barnard felt the needle again, in the other arm, tearing like a blunt knife. He tried to move to accommodate the pain, but he was bound too tight. He grunted, stretched upward, contorting his back in a small arch, fell back into the darkness.

When he was conscious again, the conversation had moved on.

'Tell me about Stenski.'

'Oh him. Not very good at it. Met him a few times in Berlin. A left-over.' If only he could stretch out his hands, grasp something solid, steady himself. Then he'd have been able to face them again. 'Give me some water.'

'When you have answered the next question: Where is Stenski now?'

'God knows.'

'If you want the water tell me.'

'They don't inform me of his movements. It's supposed to be an intelligence service, not a railway.'

'You have worked for them since 1965. You know a great many people in the service. That is inevitable. These people, they talk among themselves, they have a . . . what do you call it?'

' . . . grapevine.'

'Of course. A special word which I did

not know. A grapevine. Stenski was a senior operator. People would have discussed him. Was he given a new posting somewhere else?'

'Not my business. Keep your nose clean, they said. Concentrate on Atkins. Forget the rest.'

'But people in West Berlin must have known. At the Embassy.'

'Doubt it.'

'They must have known.' His voice altered imperceptibly. It was important, and Barnard sensed it.

'I wasn't at the Embassy much.'

'Were you not curious personally?'

'Not particularly. Why should I be?'

'A natural reaction.'

'Give me some water. You promised.'

'Water,' Karman called out.

The doctor said: 'No. Liquid is dangerous immediately after the injections.'

'Bastards,' Barnard murmured.

'That's too bad,' Karman said.

'Get lost.'

★　★　★

He woke in the cell. A headache lingered, like fragments of the interrogation. He was on the bed wearing his shirt and trousers, but none of the buttons had been done up.

Gause came, bearing a jug of water with a floral pattern on its side, and a glass. He placed them on the table, and offered them to Barnard. He came to the table in bare feet, grasped the jug in both hands, tilted it and let the rising tide of water flow into his throat. It poured from the edges of his mouth down onto the stone floor.

'You talked very freely,' Gause said. 'I thought it would take longer. Nobody can tell before, of course. It depends on the response of the drugs.'

'I remember it. You're welcome to all that gibberish.'

He had taken the jug back to the bed, and was preparing to drink again.

'Do you know what I did when I got home last night? I took down my English dictionary and I searched for a word to describe you. I found it: Abrasive.' Gause seemed rather pleased. 'I am afraid Colonel Karman is not satisfied. You talked a great deal, as I have observed, but he found you . . . abrasive. He wants to do it all again. Of course it would be more agreeable for you to consent to the interrogation without the chemical aspect.'

'I know all about you,' Barnard said. He drank heavily. 'Karman puts me through it, then you come along as the nice guy. So you get me either way. Why don't you get out of here?' He threw the jug onto the floor and swivelled his body so that he could kick it across the cell. But it had already rolled and come to rest just out of range. The water had spread away from it. 'Stagnant bloody water.'

'Karman will be harder next time. I was surprised how gentle he was with you. He even promised you water. Who would have thought Colonel Karman would ever have done that? He won't do it again.'

Barnard lay back on the bed.

'By the way, you are required to fold the blankets into a square each morning. You are not supposed to lie on the bed during the day. That is why the chair is provided.'

Barnard placed his hands behind his head and closed his eyes.

Gause moved, and Barnard thought he was going to summon people to get him off the bed; but Gause was only going out.

★　★　★

Stenski sat in a corner of the tea house. He had positioned himself opposite one of the windows, its edges leaded into the woodwork. The chairs and tables were all metal, with curved legs which ended in outstretched claws against the floor. From the window he could survey the park. To his left, the perimeter wall of the fairground, coils of barbed wire along its top; and behind, the deserted buildings of the fair; closed for the season. The ferris wheel had come to rest, and the wind played gentle games with the chairs suspended high up, rocking them to and fro like candles.

In front of him, the park: a levelled,

landscaped area with hillocks all covered in snow. Children sledged on them. Nearby, a concrete path wended its way between hillocks to a statue which was set into a rectangle cut from the earth. He could see the statue clearly, a man ten feet tall, fashioned in dull metal and wearing enormous fur boots, holding out a scroll. Johnson sat on a bench beneath the plinth, holding a Swedish newspaper. To Stenski's right the pond, frozen over. Ducks fidgeted at its edge and wandered along the concrete path which ran round it.

Johnson could see the tea house clearly. Its roof was twisted into a spiral like a basilisque; but the lace curtains prevented a view of the interior. He could see, in the opposite direction, a clock face through the trees. It was 11.35 on the Wednesday morning.

He was very cold. It had been dark when they had left the house at six that morning and made the journey to Stockholm. The wind had risen angrily against them the moment they opened the front door. He had held Andrushenko down on the bed while Stenski thrust the needle into him; they had waited by the door until Andrushenko had gone to sleep. 'We will leave him tied,' Stenski had said decisively.

In Stockholm Stenski had gone to the post office himself and left the letter — the letter addressed to Mr. Jan Olufsen of Norway and written by Andrushenko the night before. It contained directions to the tea house, and a time: 12.00. It also said: If you do not come alone, you will not see me. Signed Alexis.

Johnson had gone to the British Embassy to collect the gun and walked back to the park across a high-span bridge. The salty smell of the sea was everywhere. He had come through a square, the fountains motionless, the water in which they stood frozen as the pond. It was called Kungstradgarden and beyond it, to the east, lay a promontory with heavy old buildings on it and a car park and wharves. A ship had been moored.

In the tea house, Stenski said: 'You wait by the statue until he comes, then verify that he is alone. If he is not, do nothing. Let him come, let him go away again. If he is alone, let him enter the tea house. Then come in yourself and sit at another table near the door.'

'But I won't recognise him.'

'You will. You will sense him.'

As Stenski spoke, his eyes scanned the park.

So Johnson sat underneath the statue. The pistol felt cumbersome in his jacket pocket, all points and angles. It was too big to be carried in comfort, except in the hand. He wondered what would happen if he had to fire it; he'd had some training, but that was years ago. He hadn't handled a gun since. If he had to use it, he'd fire all eight bullets as fast as he could, and trust to the law of averages.

He had turned his coat collar up but the wind pushed at him, numbing the gloved hands which gripped the newspaper. He could hear the sound of traffic from roads which flanked the park; and once, the klaxon of an ambulance being driven fast towards the bridge.

A woman came past and walked

towards the pond. She had chunks of broken bread in a carrier bag and threw them to the ducks who were already stumbling forward to meet her.

11.46.

Johnson was moving his feet constantly, trying to keep them warm. He could hear the children on the hillock, like sounds from his own childhood: Pink cheeks, plumes of breath in the frozen air, thick gloves gripping the framework of the sledge, and the slope slipping away under his nose, faster and faster until it seemed he would never be able to stop. That was near Oxford — before the unhappy times.

11.52. He hoped Markov came on time. Otherwise, the tea house would be full of secretaries having their lunch. That would make it tricky if there was trouble. What was he supposed to do: Fire the pistol into the middle of some girls?

11.54. It was a long time, the waiting. On a sledge, going down, a minute passed as nothing; looking at the second hand of a watch, it elongated itself. His feet had smoothed the snow under the bench to a skidpan of ice. Damn the wind. It must drive those Swedes crazy, a whole winter of it, cutting through you like cold steel.

11.58.

Johnson was gazing away towards the clockface, waiting for the two hands to come together perfectly in the vertical position at midday.

Markov came from the other way. Johnson's first impulse was to stand up and do something, anything. But he watched, fascinated.

Markov moved round the pond quite casually, as if he were taking the air with a little dog. But he was alone, very much alone. His arms were short at his sides, and strong. He had no gloves. His head was bare and as bald as a Buddha. The skin of his face was furrowed.

He hesitated at the intersection between two paths and turned laboriously towards the tea house. Johnson moved, just uncrossing his legs. Markov saw him and turned, looked at him a long moment.

The man must be hyper-sensitive, feeding off everything.

He climbed the five steps to the tea house door one at a time. He was a heavy man, square and almost ungainly. He opened the door and the little bell rang once.

Then he went in.

* * *

A small room, unpainted, with nothing in it except the chair which they tied Barnard to, wrists locked behind his back, ankles to the chair legs. A little light from a feeble bulb. They had left his trousers on but removed his shirt.

Karman had a short stick.

'The drugs are very interesting,' he said. The door was padded in leather, and closed. 'You can only stand them so long, then you talk and talk and talk. But I have not the time.' He stood in front of Barnard, holding the stick horizontally at the level of his waist, a hand gripping each end. 'Something is happening,' he said. 'Something which concerns Stenski. We know a lot about him here. We have most comprehensive details of his career, his decline. He did not adapt. That is why we could break up his network. But he is doing something now, something which is very different. Almost original.' Karman had a beautiful mouth. 'I think, you see, that you know what it is, or, at least, you know where he is. You must tell me.'

'I don't know a thing.'

'We have had a telephone call. A long distance telephone call. From Moscow. They are very perturbed.' He could be civil, Karman, create a conversation, maintain it. Like Gause. 'Stenski is trying something against them. They know which country he is in. But they don't know exactly where. I promised to find out.' It was almost a point of honour. He manipulated the stick. 'And you are going to tell me.'

'Get lost.'

Barnard felt the stick across the left side of his face, two blows. He shouted, turned his face away. He felt the stick over the heart, two blows. He was scarred, but there was no blood yet. He saw the stick, held deliberately near his eyes. Another blow, on the right side of the face. He was crying.

'Where exactly is Stenski?'

* ★ ★

Johnson hesitated.

12.05.

He looked anxiously round the park. Nobody else came. The children had gone and he hadn't noticed. Markov alone: He could barely believe it.

He went quickly to the tea house.

They were sitting facing each other across the table. Johnson sat near the door, looking directly at Markov.

The Russian's eyes were grey. They encompassed everything, sharp eyes which could have been cut from precious stone.

The waitress came half way over to take Johnson's order, sensed it was the wrong moment and turned back.

'Alexis asked us to take you to him,' Stenski said. 'He would like you to know that he is very happy here.'

'He should have come himself. Why send two foreigners?' The voice was soft and controlled; nearly a whisper. Did he recognise Stenski? He must have seen a photograph in a file somewhere, sometime, even an old one. He must have done.

Johnson had his fingers wrapped round the handle of the pistol.

'Alexis has a vivid imagination,' Stenski continued. 'He thought you might not come here by yourself.'

Markov shrugged. He was calculating something slowly. 'Who is he?' He turned the grey eyes towards Johnson.

'A friend of Alexis. Like me,' Stenski said.

Markov shrugged again. 'If Andrushenko wants to meet me, we will arrange a place and time now. You can go back and tell him. But he and I, we will meet alone. No other persons present.'

Was he armed? Johnson thought of that suddenly. He had forgotten it, absolutely forgotten all about it. But his heavy hands were on the table, across the red and white cloth.

'He sends you this,' Stenski said.

Stenski laid a piece of the notepaper on the table, turning it so that Markov could read it. He did so without touching it.

Dear Sergei Markov!

You can trust these men. They are my

friends. They will bring you to me.

Markov leant forward like a big bear and brushed the paper to one side. 'Go and tell him what I have said. We will meet here tonight.'

'He won't come.' Stenski's hat lay on the table, isolated in the no-man's land between them. 'Nothing will make him. He has a great deal to lose. That is what he tells us.'

Stenski sat back and observed the park.

'I am alone,' Markov said. 'It was a bargain, and I kept my part.' Intuition: Johnson remembered Stenski's words. Markov had understood perfectly why Stenski was looking out of the window. 'Andrushenko didn't.' Markov glanced down at the piece of notepaper. It had come to rest at an angle to him. 'As for all these letters, I don't believe any of them.'

'We are only his friends, trying to help him.'

'He has been very quick to make such friends. Anyway he may be dead. Give me a telephone number and I will ring him up.'

'And trace the address afterwards.'

Markov shrugged, the big shoulders hunched.

'You've come a long way,' Stenski said, 'to back out now. All you have to do is say yes and very soon you will see him again.'

Markov thought for a moment then stood up. It was settled.

Stenski picked up his hat and put it on. He had already paid for his cup of tea. The bell rang as they went out.

Stenski and Markov walked side by side past the pond; Johnson following. They waited on the kerbside for a taxi. Nobody spoke. Johnson saw a yellow one, a Volvo, on the other side of the street and waved. The driver, heavily-bearded, swung it round and drew up in front of them.

Johnson sat in the back, next to Markov; Stenski in the front. The driver was surrounded by a clear plastic shield, moulded to the shape of his shoulders and the back of his head. 'For the drunks, on a Friday and Saturday night,' he volunteered, guessing that they were not Swedes. 'When you get them home, they don't want to pay — so they do this.' He flattened his hand, describing a rabbit punch against the neck.

'Take us out into the country,' Stenski said. 'We're visitors, and we're tired of Stockholm.'

'Where would you like to go?'

'Is there a large lake near here? I like lakes.'

'Batkyrka, that's a scenic village over-looking a very big lake. OK?'

'Yes.'

When they were on the motorway, Stenski began to peer in the driving mirror, searching for anything following.

'Lot of Germans round here,' the driver said. 'Germans and Danes. You'll see the registration plates on the cars.'

Markov was becoming impatient. 'I find this most offensive,' he said. 'I am alone. I do not expect to have to repeat that.'

They turned off 30 kilometres south and followed a side road. Then, quite suddenly, the lake stretched before them.

'What do you want to do now?' the driver asked.

'Is there a road round the lake?'

'It may not be open in winter. We can try if you want.'

The village of Batkyrka was only a few houses grouped together and they passed quickly through it. Further on, the road had been cut out of the rocks which overhung it and on the nearside, yachts had been hauled up an incline and secured there, draped in tarpaulin. Ten kilometres beyond the village, Stenski was satisfied. 'We will go back now,' he said.

The van was in a round, multi-storey carpark. All three of them sat in the front. Johnson looked at his watch before he switched the engine on: 2.35. They had plenty of time.

* * *

'One question, that is all. Where is Stenski?'

Barnard was bleeding, and the leather straps cut into the skin of his wrists. His torso was marked by the strokes of the stick, each one at a different height. He had been in the chair an hour or a moment. He smelt his own sweat from his armpits.

'Tell me.' Karman. Holding the stick in one hand, making Barnard look for it. He raised it again, high, full force. Barnard closed his eyes.

'I don't know. I'd tell you. Believe me.'

'The testicles next,' Karman said. 'We shall have to move you to a different position.'

'It's no good. I don't know.'

Barnard's hair lay in a wet matt across his forehead; that was the sweat too. 'Can't take any more,' he murmured. 'You'll beat me insensible, and I can't tell you a thing.' His head fell to one side. 'Wish I could.'

It stopped. Karman went to the door. 'Yes?' Barnard distantly heard Gause speaking. 'A telephone call? I see.' He strode out of the room.

Gause was there, with a nurse. He was almost fretting. 'I told you,' he repeated over and over again. 'I told you what it would be like.'

Barnard felt a damp, warm sponge over his face.

'Let him lie down for a few minutes,' Gause said. 'In his own room.' Barnard was conscious of the choice of that word: Room, not cell. Maybe it was just their way of talking, especially in front of a woman. Maybe something more. That was all he remembered until he woke.

He was on the bed, the blanket carefully laid over him. The nurse must have done that. Gause sat in the chair, fingering his pipe.

'Feeling better?' he said. 'I do hope so.'

Barnard traced a line from his cheekbone downwards with the index finger of his right hand. 'Christ,' he said to himself.

'Colonel Karman has told you . . . ' Gause began. 'I know what Colonel Karman has told you. About Stenski. He is in Sweden, but nobody knows what is going on up there. It is all very confused. The Russians keep ringing us up. They know you are here. They seem to think you can tell us everything.' He hesitated, unsure of how to continue, how much to say. 'Stenski has tried something completely mad. London must have sanctioned it. He could not have organised it otherwise. It would not have been an administrative possibility. The whole thing is quite . . . astonishing.'

Barnard could see the fan, spinning endlessly. His body ached.

'I made them give you something to take the pain away. It will only be effective for a certain time, but it is better than nothing,' Gause said. He stood up. 'I do not approve of what they have done to you, and I don't care who knows it. If you are going to preach humanity, practice it . . . ' Gause came closer. 'Markov. Do you know that name?'

Barnard shook his head.

'He is . . . he is a very important person in the MVD. Stenski has found some way of getting him to Sweden. The Russians knew all about that. They arranged for people to follow Markov, but something must have gone wrong. They've lost him. We wouldn't have done, but they did. You and I, we will have to make the crossing to West Berlin together. You may feel you are not fit to travel, but . . . ' He buried his pipe in his pocket. 'Shall I ask the nurse to come back and clean you up?'

Barnard nodded.

'Before she comes, we must talk. It is necessary to talk.' He came closer again. 'Who killed Atkins?' It was a rhetorical question.

'You did.'

'I have told you that that is incorrect. Unfortunately you did not believe me before. If you had done, you would have understood many things which are hidden from you. What reason did we have for killing Atkins? He was working for us, and he was useful. Nobody knew that we had turned him. We thought that. As you have observed, he did not look the kind of man who could be turned. That was partly what attracted us to him. Then he was uncovered. He must have been. I don't know the precise details yet; perhaps I never shall. But somebody found out about him, somebody on your side. Who can it have been?'

'You're talking nonsense.'

'Hardly. Who had you in West Berlin? Two men. Johnson, the tame boy who follows his master, and Stenski . . . '

Barnard opened his eyes.

'Stenski found out. I have told you: I don't know how. But it was always likely he would. He is a very suspicious man, whatever his other shortcomings may be. What then? I speculate now, and you must judge the speculation as you wish. Stenski found out, Stenski went down to the Volkspark with prior permission and beat him to death.'

'You're completely crazy.'

'No. Nobody could have guessed Stenski would do it, and when it was done, he turned round and said to London: Now there is nothing of the network left. The East Germans and Russians have broken it all up. Let us try and get Markov before I go. You have nothing to lose . . . '

Barnard was sitting up.

'I repeat: We did not kill Atkins. Why do you think we brought the woman Eva over in such a hurry? It took us by surprise.'

'McClellan must have known. He must have approved it.'

'That is what I think, also. I have spent a long time considering it. The conclusion is inescapable. I cannot say who had the idea, but I imagine it was Stenski. It would be more suited to him. So we must ask ourselves: Why did your man McClellan approve it? That is more difficult, since we know less about him. But if Stenski broke Markov, that would not reflect badly on McClellan. I think Mr. McClellan did not mention to his superiors that Stenski killed Atkins.'

Barnard had forgotten all about the pain.

'Therefore, I propose we go to West Berlin, you and I. You will telephone to London and explain what we have just discussed.'

'That won't do any good.'

'On the contrary.' Gause moved away. 'Since Stenski killed Atkins — and you might point out that Stenski knew all Atkins' habits and movements, right down to the details — there is very little reason to suppose that he will not do it again. That is why he has lured Markov to Sweden. There is another Russian there, too. He will kill them both, and Johnson won't be able to stop him.

'Stenski is like that. A prisoner of war. Much worse than Karman. He will kill as a reflex action, because of what Markov has done to him. Just like he did to Atkins. It will be a personal matter to him, quite separate from his intelligence work. London won't be expecting that, not McClellan and not the rest. They will be thinking in terms of an interrogation in Sweden, with Stenski bringing all the information back to them. You will be asking yourself why I am so keen to do all this. It is very simple. If I save two Russians, it will be very good for me. Unfortunately, we cannot ring London from East Berlin. That would be altogether implausible. You must make the call voluntarily, and from where they would expect you to make it. We can stop at the first post office on the other side. There is one very near Friedrichstrasse.'

'Good God,' Barnard said.

★   ★   ★

They reached the house at nightfall.

'Where is he?' Markov asked when they were in the hall.

'Upstairs sleeping. He is very tired.' Stenski was unconcerned now.

They went up together, Markov leading.

Markov entered the bedroom, stared at Andrushenko; noticed immediately that his hands were tied. When he turned round, Johnson had his gloves on and was holding the pistol straight at his stomach.

Markov did not raise his hands.

'You are much more stupid than I thought,' he said to Stenski. 'I cannot imagine how you ever ran a network, even a small one.'

Stenski took the pistol. Johnson remembered thinking that he wasn't wearing gloves, and his finger prints would be all over it.

Stenski backed Markov towards the bed. As Markov reached it, the side of the bed caught him behind the knees. Even as he went down, Stenski struck him with the barrel across the crown of his head, a short, precise movement with the arm travelling so quickly that Johnson barely saw it. Markov fell back and his head lay near Andrushenko's feet.

Johnson had never imagined Stenski capable of such violence. 'You might have killed him,' he said without thought.

'No.' Stenski bent over and made sure that Markov was unconscious. 'Cut a length from the tow rope, Paul, and tie him up like Andrushenko. We will carry him in the other bedroom.'

★   ★   ★

Twenty minutes later, Stenski said: 'You must go and telephone. You must inform McClellan.' He checked the time. 'Not yet six o'clock. The post office will no doubt remain open until eight, possibly later. You had better go to that town and telephone from there. It would be most unwise to telephone from anywhere nearer.'

'What about you?'

'They can do nothing. They are tied. I have this pistol. I am sure I could fire it if I needed to. This is the safety clip, and this is how you release it.' His long thumb reached up from the handle to the small catch underneath the trigger guard. 'We shall begin the interrogation when you return. Drive carefully. Don't stop for a drink anywhere. I have told you about the attitude of the Swedish police.'

As Johnson drove away, the house was in darkness save for the light from the bedroom, filtering between the closed shutters. The wind had returned, and buffeted the flat sides of the van. 6.10. He wouldn't be back for almost three hours.

He reached the main road and eased his speed up. Driving in the dark bored him and he began to sing.

Roll me over, roll me over,

Roll me over, lay me down and do it again.

★  ★  ★

Gause came back. He had left the cell door open, and Barnard took that as a sign of sincerity. 'The car is waiting in the courtyard,' he said.

Barnard was dressed. 'I look a mess,' he

said. His eyes had swollen and were almost closed. He was peering out of slits.

Gause handed him his wallet. 'We have to take them away,' he explained apologetically. 'It is standard procedure. Please check the contents. Nothing has been taken.'

'Sure,' Barnard said, drawing on his jacket. He wasn't particularly interested. 'Let's get out of here.' He had his jacket on now. 'Where's Karman? I want to spit in his face.'

'Gone home,' Gause said with great finality.

It was dark outside. Barnard had no idea of time, nor even how many days he had been captive. The car was a small one. Federal number plates.

'It's 6.40 in the evening. The rush hour will be over. That does simplify matters,' Gause said. He was a competent, careful driver. He drove back through East Berlin to the checkpoint and up to the first pole across the road. Gause showed the soldier a small plastic identification disc. The soldier stepped smartly away and lifted the pole.

'You must have influence,' Barnard said wickedly. 'It took me a bloody hour.'

They were under the arc-lamps. The speed limit was five kilometers, and Gause observed it all the way to the second pole. 'This will take a little longer,' he said. The watch tower lay ahead, monstrous in the shadows. A searchlight played over it for a moment, then its beam travelled away along the mined strip. 'Even we can't get past the second pole without the formalities.'

They got out of the car and Barnard walked stiffly behind Gause towards the passport hut.

★   ★   ★

Johnson had stopped singing, dismayed by his own voice. The van seemed to be drifting along by itself, into the night, his fingers correcting the direction with the lightest touch. He switched on the interior light to see his watch. Shortly before seven.

He would be there in a few moments. Fifteen or twenty.

Gause stood at the counter. He showed the identification card first, then the passport. The man behind the counter took the passport and pushed it through the same aperture.

'Tell them to hurry up,' Gause said. 'Tell them it's important.'

The man behind the counter wasn't going to allow some little official like Gause to dictate to him. 'If you wish to alter the procedure at the frontiers of the Democratic Republic,' he said very gravely, 'I suggest that you write to the Ministry of Foreign Affairs upon your return.'

Gause said something under his breath.

The clock on the wall moved to seven o'clock.

★ ★ ★

Johnson saw the lights of the town in the distance. The road curved and he lost them behind the trees; when he saw them again, he was only a kilometre or two away, almost where he had seen the children skiing before.

It was a sleepy town, provincial and dead. He could never contemplate living in a place like it. As he drove in he was thinking about Stenski and the pistol. That had alarmed him. Why didn't he tell Johnson to hit Markov, why did he want to do it himself? And Johnson had decided something. He was going to quit, and find some kind of life which was normal. He didn't plan to give any explanation, just tell McClellan that he was out. He would live off his mother for a while — she had money, bonds and stocks and shares, he wasn't sure how many, but enough to tide him over.

He'd write books or something.

★   ★   ★

The passports came back together. The man swivelled on his chair, lifted them from the tray into which they had fallen and placed them a distance apart on the counter.

Gause hurried back to the car.

Two soldiers already stood beside it, one leaning against a low trolley on which was mounted a mirror. When Gause was present, he slid it underneath the car and looked earnestly at the mirror to make sure nobody was hiding there. The other soldier was pulling the rear seats forward, probing with a stick. Gause stood close by, Barnard further away.

The searchlight played across their faces as it dipped. Barnard lifted a hand to shield his eyes, but before he was able to do so, the beam had moved away. Somebody shifted in the watch-tower and surveyed them through binoculars. Clockwork people, Barnard thought again.

The soldiers went away.

Gause drove through at a slow and respectful speed.

\*   \*   \*

Johnson parked the van in the square. On the ground floor of one of the buildings, he could see a bar and people drinking at tables. That was exactly what he wanted to put into his life: The unthinking

346

normality of going out in the evening and having a drink. Meeting people, listening to a few jokes. Trying to pull the barmaid.

'And don't stop for a drink anywhere,' Stenski had said.

Johnson couldn't decide whether to go over and have a drink simply in defiance. Sit at a table for half an hour and just order a beer. He turned towards the post office. Its door was open, its lights on. He was almost disappointed. If it had been closed, that would have given him the pretext for the beer.

He walked slowly towards it.

* * *

There were two men in the hut on the western side. Barnard handed both passports through the passenger window. They were checked in a moment and returned.

'I'll talk to McClellan all right,' Barnard said. 'You know he wanted to pull me off it, after I got beaten up? Know why? Because I was getting too damn close. I could decimate him now if I wanted.' He glanced across at Gause. They were up at the other end of Friedrichstrasse, and he was turning left. 'I thought it might have appealed to you.'

But Gause would not be drawn on that.

★ ★ ★

Johnson was inside the post office. The woman behind the grille was knitting again.

'London?' she queried. She remembered his face.

He nodded, and told her the number. Her English was good enough, and he couldn't see the point in writing it down again. Either way, it wasn't a security consideration. He went to cabin one without being told. The knitting lay on her lap, and she dialled intently.

It won't take a minute, he thought. One thing about these Swedes: They're quick.

'All lines to London are engaged,' she said apologetically. 'I will try again in a moment.'

★ ★ ★

The post office near Friedrichstrasse was in a modern building with swing doors. It was carpeted in some green, synthetic material which did not give under the feet. A girl sat at an information desk.

'Calls abroad?' Gause said quickly.

She pointed to another desk in an annex. A man was there with a telephone in front of him. Along the walls were arranged glass cubicles and some Arabs were squatted down on the bench which ran down the middle of the room, waiting for their calls. A large woman sat away from them, reading a magazine.

Barnard asked for the number. The man noted it on a pad and told them to sit down. 'You will be called,' he observed. To the left of the telephone, he had a microphone on a small plastic mounting.

'It's urgent,' Barnard said.

'I can't make them go any faster,' the man said heatedly. It was seven fifteen. No doubt he had had a long and difficult day, especially with the Arabs.

*   *   *

'Still engaged.' The woman seemed surprised. 'We have fewer lines in the evening, that's the reason, I suppose.' She resumed knitting. It was a pullover for a child.

'Daughter?' Johnson asked. He had positioned himself near the grille. He wanted to talk to somebody.

The woman shook her head. 'For a cousin.'

Johnson envied her: The family, the job . . .

'I do have a daughter,' the woman said, knitting while she talked. 'But she has grown up now. She will marry in the spring.'

\* \* \*

'London.' The man stooped his head, and spoke into the microphone from the side of his mouth. 'Cabin seven.' The Arabs had looked up hopefully, and now talked among themselves.

Barnard and Gause went into the cabin together. There was hardly enough room for them. Barnard picked up the receiver.

350

'Your London call.'

'McClellan, please.' It was humid, dry and hot, in the cabin, and Barnard wished he'd taken off his coat.

'Connecting you.' A woman on the switchboard in London; Barnard didn't recognise her voice.

'McClellan.' He announced himself in his clipped Scottish way, cloaking himself in dignity.

'Barnard here.'

'Where have you been?'

'Never mind now.'

And Gause whispered: 'We could be too late. It might be all over.'

'You listen to me, McClellan,' Barnard said. 'Listen and don't interrupt.'

'Where are you speaking from?'

'Just listen. I haven't the time or the patience for any stupid questions.' Barnard was sweating, and his eyes were sore. Damn the overcoat. 'I've been doing what I came here to do, and I've found something out. Stenski is in Sweden. It's the talk of Berlin. Everybody here knows, and that includes the MVD. Got that?'

351

'Yes.' McClellan sacrificed none of his calmness, none of the monotone as he uttered the single word. But Barnard was calculating that it must have been a hell of a shock.

'Wait. There's more. Stenski killed Atkins, and that is common knowledge, too. Did you hear that clearly?'

Barnard could feel Gause edging closer, wanting to miss no part of the conversation.

'And now the old crank has got a couple of Russians up with him in Sweden and the MVD people are sure he is going to kill them. I only found out tonight.' Barnard paused to wipe the sweat away. His sleeve brushed his eyelids, and he remembered the beating. 'The Russians are looking for him at this minute. And his side-kick.'

'You say nothing about this to anybody,' McClellan began. But Barnard cut him short.

'That's just it, you see. I will have to make a full report.' The welts on Barnard's chest were beginning to ache again, and he felt short of breath. 'But for

Christ's sake stop Stenski killing them.'

'Where are you speaking from?'

'A post office.'

'Totally irresponsible. I am not surprised. Your whole mode of operation is the same.'

'Don't lecture me.' Barnard was shouting. But he knew McClellan was playing for time, doing his own calculations.

'Take the first aeroplane home in the morning. I presume there is not one tonight. If you do not, you will be instantly dismissed.'

'Can you still stop Stenski?'

'That is no concern of yours.'

★  ★  ★

They did not speak until they were back in the car.

'We'll have to wait and see,' Barnard said. 'Unless my eyes go on swelling. Then I won't be able to see a thing.' He laughed roughly.

Gause was gazing absently along the street.

'Where shall I drop you?' he asked.

'The airport or the Embassy?' He was very calm.

'A hospital, the way I feel.'

*  ★  ★

'Ah, the lines are clear, cabin one.' Johnson moved quickly. 'London are there now.'

'McClellan, please.' Johnson waited.

'Putting you through.'

'McClellan.'

Of course he would be there, even at half past seven at night. He'd stayed, anticipating that either Johnson or Stenski would ring with a progress report.

'Johnson here.' It was too late for the bogus mumbo-jumbo of codes and passwords. Johnson was getting out, anyway.

'Where are you?'

'A post office.'

'Do not on any account put the telephone down until I instruct you to. Have you transferred the charge?'

'What are you talking about?'

'I want to know if you are likely to be

cut off. If we are paying at this end, you will not be.'

'No, I haven't but they won't cut me off. The system is not like that here. You pay after the call is over.'

'I see. What is happening?'

'We have two guests with us now, I am happy to say.'

'The expected guests?'

'Yes.' Johnson half-covered the mouth-piece with his hand, just as a precaution. 'The second guest arrived safely today.'

'Congratulations. Unfortunately . . . there have been complications.' McClellan paused, and Johnson sensed he was hesitating, unsure of what to say next. 'The word is out. Do you understand?' His voice rose in intensity, and Johnson could never remember hearing McClellan like that. 'They are looking for you. Perhaps they are very close.' He was talking quickly and urgently, careless of the construction of the sentences. 'How long will it take you to drive back to the house?'

'One hour and fifteen minutes. That's about my average.'

'As long as that?'

'Yes. The roads are icy, and . . . '

'Quite so. Quite so.' McClellan was excited. 'Drive back now and instruct Stenski to do nothing, absolutely nothing. No interrogation, nothing. Release your guests anywhere, at a railway station, anywhere. Then take Stenski to the British Embassy in Stockholm tonight. Tonight. I will inform the Embassy that you are coming. Stay strictly within the Embassy confines. Tell Stenski that it is an instruction.' He paused again. 'Disregard his reaction. Further — force him to go to the Embassy, if that is necessary. I give you authority to do it. Do you understand?'

'What's going on?'

'Drive as fast as you can now. Without killing yourself, of course.' He added that as a distant afterthought.

'Listen . . . '

'Do as you are told. There is little enough time, perhaps no time at all. Everybody in Berlin knows about it, and enough people in Moscow as well. The whole thing's gone wrong.' McClellan stopped talking, but he hadn't finished. Johnson knew that; McClellan was being carried along by some kind of desperate impetus, and it hadn't spent itself yet. 'Stenski is a dangerous man. I shall not repeat that. When you get back to the house, you watch him carefully. Did you get the firearm from the Embassy?'

'Yes.'

'I strongly recommend that you carry it, and not he.'

'Good God.'

'Who has it at present?'

'He has.'

'That may be difficult. I am sure you can persuade him to give it to you if you are discreet enough. Tell him . . . tell him anything but get it and keep it away from him. That is an order also. Now put this telephone down and go. Do not let Stenski overrule you, do not let him intimidate you. You've got to be a man about it. Telephone me in the morning from the Embassy.'

'I don't understand — but I've a right to understand. I'm getting tired of being treated . . . '

'Your guests are not safe alone with him. What do you want me to do — spell it out? Come on, boy, can't you see I'm trying to help us all?'

'I'm going now.'

He hurried to the van when he had paid the woman, fumbled with the keys. Singing was coming from the bar, and he looked across at the warm, inviting lights for the last time.

He knew it was useless to hurry, because he knew Stenski. The two-way journey took two and a half hours, plus the time for the call. Stenski would have timed it when Johnson went the time before to buy the food.

But he drove as fast as he could.

He was unarmed, but that was wholly irrelevant. He could no more have used the pistol on Stenski than himself. They would both understand that.

The road stretched before him, lonely and bare. No traffic came towards him. He thought he might clip ten minutes off the return, not more. Out of three hours, what did that add up to? It was too late.

Once the van drifted on a corner and

went into a slide, slithering towards the pine trees at the roadside. He let it go without manipulating the steering wheel to correct it or touching the brakes. He knew what brakes would do on ice. He waited until it had slewed and slowed, then eased it gently back.

He was thankful for the deserted road. It would have been nasty if another vehicle had been approaching.

The journey seemed to take a long time, and as he got nearer, his apprehension grew.

He saw the lake. The moon was behind the clouds, incandescent on the water. He saw the house, on the promontory, isolated and in complete darkness.

The van lurched along the tapering path towards it and he stopped twenty yards from the front door and extinguished the headlamps. Nothing moved. He could hear only the wind against the shutters, a frenzied, aching, godless howl.

He climbed down from the van and stood beside it, motionless; he was frightened. Snow brushed against his feet, skimmed from the ice round the lake.

He walked slowly to the front door. It was not locked. He opened it and hesitated. He wished he had the pistol. He turned to make sure nobody was behind him. On the far hillside, a pine tree at the spur of the hill had been decorated with fairy lights. He noticed them, turned again, and went into the hall. He felt for the light switch along the wall, found it, turned it on.

The hall was empty.

'Stenski,' Johnson called it out weakly, as if he might almost have wished for no reply.

The front door moved and he turned, startled. That was only the wind.

'Stenski.'

The wood creaked as he mounted, step by step. Before he gained the landing, he saw that both bedroom doors were open.

He did not need to switch on any more lights. The one in the hall was strong enough.

Through the left hand door, he could see the foot of the bed and blood on the floorboards, static but not yet seeped into the wood. He went in. Andrushenko had

360

died quickly. A blow or two had been enough. His eyes were open, pink and sightless, and blood was gathered at the rim of the eyelids. Johnson backed away and turned, facing the other bedroom. The bed was behind the door and against the far wall. He could see nothing unless he entered.

You're a man, McClellan had said. Johnson could hear him saying it again like a distant, comfortless echo.

So enter the bedroom, prove your manhood.

Markov lay by the bed wearing his coat. His forehead had been battered and beaten and lacerated. His left arm was broken and almost dismembered. His mouth swollen. His hands were still tied behind his back. Johnson had done that. Stenski's suitcase was gone.

He thought for an instant of Atkins.

Then he felt the saliva gather in his mouth and he wanted to vomit.

He couldn't remember, even moments later, whether he had walked or run back down the stairs. The wind had closed the front door. He pulled it open and stepped out. The snow drifted toward his feet like angry hands seeking to touch him.

He saw the tree again, in the distance; saw the necklace of red and blue and white lights woven around it. He understood.

It was Christmas Eve.

## THE END